"You look so beautiful."

James's eyes had that drenched look they always had after they'd made love, Mattie thought. They couldn't keep their hands off each other. But beautiful? Well, she did her best. The russet-colored silk dress she was wearing was one of the "must haves" her friend had insisted she buy all those months ago. Soon she wouldn't be able to get into it.

Which was why she hadn't wanted to come here tonight. She needed to tell James she was pregnant.

D0837811

DIANA HAMILTON is a true romantic and fell in love with her husband at first sight. They still live in the fairy-tale Tudor house where they raised their three children. Now the idyll is shared with eight rescued cats and a puppy. But despite an often chaotic lifestyle, ever since she learned to read and write Diana has had her nose in a book—either reading or writing one—and plans to go on doing just that for a very long time to come.

Books by Diana Hamilton

HARLEQUIN PRESENTS®
2132—BOUGHT: ONE HUSBAND
2178—CLAIMING HIS WIFE

Don't miss any of our special offers. Write to us at the following address for information on our newest releases.

Harlequin Reader Service
U.S.: 3010 Walden Ave., P.O. Box 1325, Buffalo, NY 14269
Canadian: P.O. Box 609, Fort Erie, Ont. L2A 5X3

Diana Hamilton

THE CHRISTMAS CHILD

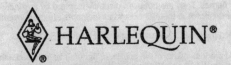

TORONTO • NEW YORK • LONDON
AMSTERDAM • PARIS • SYDNEY • HAMBURG
STOCKHOLM • ATHENS • TOKYO • MILAN • MADRID
PRAGUE • WARSAW • BUDAPEST • AUCKLAND

If you purchased this book without a cover you should be aware
that this book is stolen property. It was reported as "unsold and
destroyed" to the publisher, and neither the author nor the
publisher has received any payment for this "stripped book."

ISBN 0-373-12221-7

THE CHRISTMAS CHILD

First North American Publication 2001.

Copyright © 2000 by Diana Hamilton.

All rights reserved. Except for use in any review, the reproduction or
utilization of this work in whole or in part in any form by any electronic,
mechanical or other means, now known or hereafter invented, including
xerography, photocopying and recording, or in any information storage
or retrieval system, is forbidden without the written permission of the
publisher, Harlequin Enterprises Limited, 225 Duncan Mill Road,
Don Mills, Ontario, Canada M3B 3K9.

All characters in this book have no existence outside the imagination of
the author and have no relation whatsoever to anyone bearing the same
name or names. They are not even distantly inspired by any individual
known or unknown to the author, and all incidents are pure invention.

This edition published by arrangement with Harlequin Books S.A.

® and TM are trademarks of the publisher. Trademarks indicated with
® are registered in the United States Patent and Trademark Office, the
Canadian Trade Marks Office and in other countries.

Visit us at www.eHarlequin.com

Printed in U.S.A.

CHAPTER ONE

'SO IT'S going to be your usual quiet Christmas,' Dawn stated from the depths of the armchair which was cosily close to the state-of-the-art kitchen range. 'Poor old you! You really should learn to have fun, Matts—you never know, you might get to like it!' Her soft, pretty mouth formed a small moue of condemnation as she wriggled her curvy body with barely suppressed excitement and Mattie, glancing across at her oldest and best friend, wondered if her mother would have loved her if she'd been more like Dawn, pretty and curvy, outgoing and bubbly, instead of—

She pushed the thought roughly away. All that was over. Her mother had died nine years ago, for heaven's sake, when Mattie had been just sixteen and there was no point at all in dwelling on the past—nothing would bring it back, or alter it.

'Whereas your place will be bursting at the seams,' Mattie put in through a gentle smile, sensing her friend's excitement and knowing the reason for it. She reached for her reading glasses and peered at the recipe book. At Christmas time especially, The Old Rectory on the other side of the picture-book Sussex village would act like a magnet for the large and happily uncomplicated family Dawn's parents had created. And the rambling, slightly shabby house would be filled with children and grandchildren, love and laughter.

In stark contrast to the rather austere grandeur of this place, the home she shared with her widowed father.

'The whole shooting match,' Dawn agreed comfortably, her hazel eyes bright as she raised her left hand and gazed at the emerald sparkling on her ring finger. 'Plus Frank and his parents,' she added breathily. 'They'll be arriving tomorrow, Christmas Eve, so you're invited for lunch on Christmas Day—bring your father—with Mrs Flax being away it will save you having to cook. And I won't take no for an answer. I can't wait to introduce my brand-new fiancé to my very best friend.'

'Sorry.' Mattie fed flour onto the kitchen scales. 'But James is spending the holiday here; he phoned this morning and invited himself.' Her heart squeezed painfully beneath her breast as she spoke his name. He must be feeling dreadful. His plans for Christmas would have been far more glamorous, much more romantic than a quiet few days out in the sticks. 'I know you're going to say bring him too, but I don't think he'll feel like partying—not under the circumstances.'

More than half expecting her friend to persist, she tipped the flour into the mixing bowl with such a gesture of finality that airy clouds of it rose palely to the ceiling.

But far from insisting that her invitation be accepted, Dawn said, 'Wow!' wriggling round in the chair, resting her elbows on the fatly padded arm, cupping her chin in her hands. 'Major tear-mopping time coming up?'

'I don't think James Carter knows how to cry,' Mattie stated, her tone matter-of-fact. In all the years she had known him, as the son of her father's business partner, and later, at the relatively young age of twenty-five, stepping into his father's shoes at his death around eleven years ago, she had never seen him show a strong emotion. He was always self-assured, completely collected, detached. Almost frighteningly remote at times, seeming to live in a world where nothing could touch him.

But right now he must be hurting. Being so publicly jilted by the woman he'd intended to marry had to be a painful experience. But, knowing him as well as she did, she was sure he wouldn't show it.

'Well, he wouldn't parade his feelings in public,' Dawn conceded. 'But with his parents both dead now, you and your dad are the closest thing to a family he has, so he might cry on your shoulders. And I guess his ego has taken a heck of a pounding if nothing else. I mean, when you look back a couple of months to those burblings in the gossip columns about the wedding of the year—"Society Beauty, the Hon. Fiona Campbell-Blair to Wed Business Tycoon," and her quoted as saying it would be a marriage made in heaven and how besotted with each other they were, and then, only last week her ladyship announces that she's called the whole thing off because, and again I quote, "Jimmy didn't live up to her high expectations"—well, I mean, he's got to be feeling absolutely gutted.'

'Probably,' Mattie responded tightly, wishing her friend would drop the subject. She hated to think of James being hurt and she wanted to take the wretched Fiona's elegant neck in her own two hands and do her a serious damage! And she couldn't imagine any woman who wasn't certifiably insane jilting a man who was as starkly, compellingly male as James Carter.

'Look,' she suggested, 'why don't you make coffee?' Anything to stop this post-mortem prattling. She peered again at the recipe book and began rubbing butter into the flour. 'I'm trying to make pastry for mince pies here. I just wish Mrs Flax hadn't decided to take her annual leave right now!'

When their housekeeper had announced she wanted a winter break in the sun with her sister she had had their blessing. Mattie's dad had never liked the festive season—not after his wife, Mattie's mother, had walked out on them all those years ago—so they tended to treat Christmas as just another ordinary day. But with James expected she was going to produce all the trimmings. Even if it killed her!

'Consider it done.' Dawn unwound herself and wandered over to the table, casting her eyes over the recipe Mattie was so laboriously following. 'It says add water, but you'll get a much nicer result if you use beaten egg instead,' she advised. 'Want me to take over? I've been helping Mum with the cooking practically since I was born and you're nothing but an academic. Brainy but a total fluff-head when it comes to anything practical.'

'Then it's time I mended my ways,' Mattie responded lightly, resisting the impulse to clutch the mixing bowl jealously to her under-endowed chest. She couldn't do much for James—she had enough common sense to be fully aware of that—but she could and she would, and with her own hands, make a proper Christmas for him.

'On your own head be it—or should I say on your guest's stomach lie it!'

Mattie grimaced wryly as her friend swung away to fill the kettle. Although only a couple of weeks separated them in age, she sometimes felt a thousand years old around the ebullient Dawn. A point reinforced when the other girl tossed over her shoulder, 'Play your cards right, Matts, and you could catch him on the rebound.'

Mattie dropped the rolling-pin on the floured board as a savage pain thrust its jagged way through her. Closely followed by a searing anger that made her voice dagger-sharp. 'Sometimes, Dawn, you talk like a particularly stupid ten-year-old!'

James Carter wouldn't look twice at the plain, insignificant Matilda Trent. He went for the beautiful ones, the stylishly elegant ones. Women like his ex-fiancée. Women who stood out in a crowd, not ones who faded into the wallpaper. Dawn had to know that; how could she not?

'If you say so.' Unfazed by the rebuke, Dawn brewed coffee. 'But think about it. Before I went to work in Richmond the two of us were practically joined at the hip, which means, of course, that I saw him almost as often as you did.' She reached for mugs from the dresser, found the milk and sugar. 'Around you, he always seemed sort of—protective, gentle. It's difficult to put a finger on it, but there's definitely a healthy dollop of affection there. And after being dumped by that high-class, empty-headed trollop he's going to appreciate someone who's intelligent, loyal, nice to know, calm. You fell in love with him eleven whole years ago when you were fourteen, you know you did, so go for it, Matts.'

Calm! She was seething! Dawn had stuck a knife between her ribs and was blithely twisting it—too insensitive to imagine how much it was hurting!

Golden eyes narrowing behind her lenses, Mattie snapped, 'I got a crush on James around the same time you "fell in love" with our science master, remember? I grew out of it before you switched your eternal devotion to some mangy pop star or other! So drop it, will you?'

Only the trouble was, she was lying—she hadn't grown out of it at all. She'd tried to, heaven knew she had. But her feelings for James, kept secret for so long now, had stubbornly refused to do anything but grow until they were positively awesome.

James slid from behind the wheel of the Jaguar, locked it and pocketed the key. A million stars patterned the winter night sky and the frosty air bit into his lungs as he pulled in a deep breath and felt himself begin to relax. Despite the turmoil going on in his life he could still recognise the magic of Christmas Eve. Strange, that.

Lights glowed dimly from a couple of curtained windows, but otherwise the stately bulk of Berrington House was in darkness. On the drive out from London he'd been having second thoughts about the wisdom of spending the festive season with the Trents. But standing here, in the silence, he knew he'd been right to invite himself to stay for two or three days.

After the messy drama of the past week it was what he needed. The flavour of that final scene with the woman he'd decided to marry was a sour taste in his mouth. And as for what had happened—unconsciously, he shrugged wide, hard-boned shoulders, the twist of his mouth cynical—he could understand why Fiona had gone to the press even though he deplored the way she'd made the break-up so damned public.

He needed to put the whole humiliating and painful episode behind him, and he could do it here.

Over the years, this house had come to represent a second home to him, both he, and his father before him, preferring to talk business over a civilised dinner or long weekend with Edward Trent, co-partner in their now huge construction empire.

It wasn't the house itself—Berrington was a touch too severe for his taste, more like a showcase for traditional perfection than a lived-in home. Neither was it his partner's company that had drawn him here, at this time.

It was Mattie, he recognised now. Her undemanding presence was exactly what he needed.

His frown darkened. That admission wasn't something he was happy with. He'd learned to be self-sufficient at an early age. He didn't want to need what another living soul could give him.

But her impressive intelligence stimulated him, her serenity soothed him, and her foibles—such as her complete inability to master anything vaguely practical—gently amused him. It had taken her months to learn how to use the word processor he'd finally persuaded her to install and eight failed attempts to pass her driving test. Even now, she was the worst driver he knew.

Then there was her refreshing lack of female vanity—she had to be the least clothes-conscious woman born, the least sexually aware. She didn't suffer from fluttering eyelashes, siren pouts, come-bed-me glints seductively shafted from sultry eyes.

That, he worked out with a surge of relief, was what he really needed: the company of a woman who didn't throw out sexual challenges, who didn't attract him physically, and didn't want to.

Mouse. The hard slash of his mouth softened fractionally. Dear old Mouse.

Tightening his grip on his overnight bag, he strode over the perfectly raked gravel, heading for the main door, wondering, apropos of nothing in particular, whether she was still struggling with the intricacies of translating that bulky scientific tome from the original German to Italian or whether it was done and dusted, back with the publisher, put safely to bed.

He was confident it would be the latter; he knew his Mattie. Financially, she had no need to work, but once she had a project on the go she tended not to surface until it was completed. Perfectly. As soon as she answered to his ring, he'd ask.

But it was his partner who opened the door. For a man nearing his sixties his face was relatively unlined, personable, only his iron-grey hair and thickening waistline betraying his age. And his eyes were betraying his embarrassment.

Edward Trent wasn't comfortable with emotions. If he had any he kept them firmly locked away and expected everyone he came in contact with to do likewise. James was the same in that respect, which was probably why they worked so well together.

Best get it out of the way.

'Good of you to give me houseroom for a day or two,' James stated, walking over the threshold. 'I felt the need to go to ground for a while. But I'm not going to bore you with all the gory details, or get maudlin over the port. So I suggest we put the whole subject of my publicly broken engagement under wraps.'

'Best thing.' Edward gave an audible huff of relief. 'Though before we drop it, I'll tell you you're well out of it. As you know, Mattie and I only met her once but we both agreed she wasn't good enough for you. A fine pedigree, granted. And she'd have made a first-rate hostess, and now you've taken over the reins of the company that's something you need. But the woman's shallow, selfish, hard. It would never have worked out. That said, would you like to go to your room and freshen up, or join me in a drink before supper?'

'I'll settle for that drink,' James agreed tautly, feeling his blood pressure rise. He dropped his overnight bag at the foot of the broad staircase and followed his host into an immaculately kept, minimally furnished sitting room.

So Mattie hadn't thought Fiona good enough for him! What the hell did she know about it? he derided savagely. In his opinion his partner's daughter didn't live in the real world, holed up here in her ivory tower backwater, dedicated to her work, a total innocent, ignorant of what went on between adult, sexually active men and women.

She had no right to pass judgement.

As far as he knew she had no sex life, so how could she possibly begin to understand the male ache to possess a woman as beautiful, as sinfully provocative as the Fionas of this world—the desire to have such a woman share his bed, grace his table at the many business dinners he was forced to host, run his home and his social diary with clockwork precision?

Aware that he was scowling, he forced himself to lighten up as he accepted the generous measure of single malt Edward handed him, sank into one of the stiffly upholstered chairs arranged around a rather fine Chippendale tripod table and asked, 'Where's Mattie?' the unprecedented anger at her temerity in passing judgement on something she knew damn-all about beginning to fade with the first gulp of excellent liquor.

In any case, it had been an unworthy emotion. He hadn't directed his anger at Edward who had expressed the same opinion, had he? The events of the last week must have affected him more than he'd realised.

'Flapping around in the kitchen,' Edward replied. 'With Mrs Flax being away it's going to be very much a case of pot luck, I'm afraid. Outside her work, Matilda's as organised as a parcel of two-year-olds lost in a maze.'

James took another comforting mouthful of whisky. Poor Mattie! He'd foisted his company on them and he knew darned well that, without him, they'd have settled for bread and cheese or something out of a tin until the housekeeper returned. He wasn't going to let her get stressed out on his behalf. Over the next day or so he'd help her. They'd share the load. The decision surprised him, but he'd stick with it.

Far from flapping around in the kitchen, Mattie was in her bedroom staring gloomily at her reflection. When she'd heard the sounds of James' arrival she'd become horribly aware of the way her jeans and sloppy sweatshirt had suffered throughout a long morning spent, not very successfully, in the kitchen, followed by the afternoon scramble in the woods that backed onto their gardens, cutting holly to decorate the dining room.

But she didn't look a whole lot more appealing in the soft brown skirt and fawn sweater she'd changed into. Still damp from the quick shower she'd taken, her shoulder-length chestnut-coloured hair looked almost black as she screwed it back in its usual bunch at the nape of her neck. And her skin was too pale and there was nothing she could do about the peculiar yellow colour of her eyes.

Frowning, she turned from the mirror and collected her discarded clothes for the laundry. There was no point whatsoever in using make-up. She knew she was plain, had always known it. And no amount of staring at her reflection would alter an unremarkable nose, a jaw that was too wide or a mouth that was too fat!

James wouldn't notice if she served dinner dressed in a sack. Mouse, that was what he sometimes called her. That was the way he saw her. Something small, quiet, grey. Insignificant. She knew all that, didn't she? Had accepted the stark truth of it years ago. Why the self-critical appraisal now?

So get a grip, she admonished herself tartly. He'd never done a single thing to encourage the way she felt about him. Was—heaven be praised—totally unaware of the deep-rooted emotions she had where he was concerned. So deep-rooted that she'd never once actually noticed any other man, not in that way, had never been tempted to follow the example of her friends at university and indulge in casual affairs.

Instead of mooning over what could never be she should be down there, trying, in her own quiet way, to offer him kindness and understanding over the next few days, hopefully doing something to help ease the anguish of his broken heart.

Stoically ignoring the pain in her own heart, she lifted her chin, straightened her spine and hurried downstairs.

'Of course I'm going to help prepare lunch,' James stated unequivocally the next morning. 'I don't expect to be waited on hand and foot. Besides...' one dark brow arched humorously '...neither of us has fixed a full-scale Christmas lunch before; the results could be fun.'

Mattie bit down on her lower lip. Hard. Did he have to look so rivetingly gorgeous? Did her wretched insides have to go into spasm whenever he was around?

Dressed this morning in hip-hugging, narrow grey trousers and a casual black cashmere sweater that displayed a breadth of shoulder that just invited a girl to snuggle into, he was six-two of male perfection. Top that by the austerity of hard-boned features, and silvery-grey eyes made sultry by heavy lids and lashes that were as thick and black as his hair and you got an endlessly fascinating combination.

Stop it! she growled inside her head. Think of something else. Anything.

'If you're afraid of a repeat performance of last night's supper, don't be,' she said as lightly as she could. It had been a complete disaster. 'The quiche was soggy, the salad still had bugs in it and the mince pies were about as edible as lumps of tarmac.'

She was wearing one of Mrs Flax's cotton overalls and it swamped her. Pulling her reading glasses out of a capacious side pocket, she fixed them on her nose. Looking as she did, like someone kitted out for the frump-of-the-year show, was some sort of protection. It served to drive home the fact, emphasise it, that in his book she would never be worth a second glance.

Reputedly ruthless in business, he had always been kind to her—when he'd got around to noticing her. But that was all. Absolutely all. Sometimes she thought he actually found her amusing and at others he didn't seem to see her, looking through her, rather than at her.

Pulling in a deep breath, she rallied, explaining soberly, 'Fact is, I panicked. Did everything wrong. Because Mrs Flax does all the cooking I've never had to learn. But that doesn't mean I can't. It has to be entirely a matter of logic and planning. So I sat up last night and made lists, read cookery books, assembled—' Aware that his gorgeous eyes were sending dancing silver glints in her direction, she broke off, adding tartly, 'I've got the whole operation planned, down to the last frozen sprout.'

The exercise had left her with bags under her eyes but had at least taken her mind off the fact that he was sleeping under the same roof. Or not sleeping, lying awake, mourning his lost love. 'And I'm sure you could spend the morning more profitably with Dad. I know he's eager to discuss the funding of the hotel complex project in Spain—or was it Italy?'

'Spain,' he said. 'And that can wait.' She looked

so earnest, her hair scraped back from her plain little face, her owly glasses slipping down to the end of her neat little nose, her golden eyes serious. She was bringing her impressive thought processes to bear on the problem in hand.

Bravo Mattie!

'Nevertheless, I'm going to help you. If nothing else, I can peel potatoes, supply you with coffee, mop your fevered brow. I promise you, I shall enjoy it. Enjoy your company.'

And that was the truth. It didn't surprise him in the least. Mattie was always comfortable to be around. And watching her grapple with alien practicalities—the way her quirky brows would pull together with a frown of concentration, the pink tip of her tongue peep from the corners of her mouth, just as it had done when she had been trying to master the mysteries of her word processor—would amuse him, would take his mind off—off other things.

'If that's what you really want.' Mattie pretended to consult the lengthy list she'd left on the butcher's block table. He wouldn't enjoy it. He would know that the makings of a huge Christmas lunch that Mrs Flax had left in the deep freeze would have stayed right there if he hadn't invited himself here. He was doing what he would see as his duty.

She would not let herself believe that he really did enjoy being with her. She wasn't into self-delusion. But James, in this warmer, noticing mood was dangerous stuff.

And went on being dangerous to her equilibrium right through the holiday, his easy charm taking her breath away, making her sometimes believe in that old chestnut that if you wanted something badly enough it came to you. Only occasionally did he seem to withdraw into darkness, his eyes deeply thoughtful, brooding, she was sure of it, on his lost love. Not that Fiona's name had been mentioned, not once.

This morning, the day James was due to leave, her father had taken himself off for a walk, complaining that he'd eaten far too much. 'You did us proud, Mattie,' he'd said, sounding astonished. And then, as if inner enlightenment had been granted, 'But then, James was around to see you didn't go dishing up any more disasters!'

Mattie resented that, she really did. She'd worked hard to bring some sort of logic to the mysteries of turning basic raw ingredients into palatable meals. She deserved some credit, she thought grumpily as she pushed the vacuum cleaner around the house with more passion than purpose and was thrusting it back into its cupboard in the kitchen when James walked in.

'Ready to go?' She sounded calm, sensible. Inside she was a mess. She would miss him dreadfully. She probably wouldn't see him again for months. Only last night she'd happened, in passing the sitting-room door, to hear her father tell him that he'd travel up to the London head office in a day or two to discuss the funding for the Spanish project with him and their company accountant. So he wouldn't be dropping by in the near future.

'Almost.' He closed the door behind him and leaned against it, his arms folded over his chest, as if barring her exit. Mattie took one look at him—he was so beautiful, even the worn old denim jeans and ancient leather jacket couldn't detract from the lean, powerful elegance of his tall, whippy frame—and looked swiftly away.

She really did have to stop thinking this way. She'd managed to keep her emotions off the boil for years, tucking them away, refusing to let them churn her up. She could do it again. Hell's teeth, of course she could!

Closing the cupboard door, she turned again to face him, smoothing down the smothering folds of the unflattering borrowed overall.

'Can I get you a coffee before you go?' That was better—she'd subdued the painful lump in her chest that might have made speech impossible. She was back to being calm and helpful.

'Not for me.' He levered his hard frame away from the door, walked towards her, his silver eyes intent. 'There's something I want to ask you. And before you jump down my throat, I want you to consider it carefully, bring your usual unruffled intelligence into play.'

He stopped walking, left a few feet of space between them, smiling wryly as that well-known puzzled little frown appeared between her eyes. The idea had come to him suddenly, and it was a good one. He'd thought about it long and hard since it had occurred to him last night, after his discussion with Edward.

It made good, practical sense. And he knew his Mattie. Once she got used to the thought of having to uproot herself she would see that.

'Mattie,' he said levelly. 'Will you marry me?'

CHAPTER TWO

SOMETHING scary had happened to her, Mattie thought wildly. A sudden rush of blood to her head, maybe? It had boiled her brain, sent her loopy, made her hear things.

James proposing? To her?

'Mattie?'

Even through the shock of fearing herself to have suffered a mortal affliction, she was bright enough to detect a note of wry amusement when she heard one. So that was it. A joke. An unfunny joke.

Oh, how dared he? It would serve him right if she took him seriously, flung herself at him, dewy-eyed and babbling about big white wedding dresses and having his babies. All those barren, hopeless years of loving this man didn't stop her from wanting to punish him!

But common sense eventually did just that. Pretending to take him seriously would hurt her more than it hurt him. Winding her arms around him, covering his face with kisses, would be torture.

She uprooted her feet from the floor and trudged to the sink to fill the kettle. She needed coffee, even if he didn't. At least she was moving now, thinking clearly. She said flatly, 'Be careful, James. Jokes like that could rebound on you. You might be taken seriously.'

'I meant it, Matts,' he said from right behind her.

She froze. Everything inside her turned into stone. This was not possible. How could he mean it?

Lifting his hands, he took her shoulders, turning her to face him, and that brought her to life, blood coursing madly through her veins at his touch. She shrugged his hands away. He had never touched her before, not even accidentally, and much as she might crave this small intimacy she couldn't handle it, not right now, not if she were to find out what his agenda was.

'Has this got something to do with Fiona dumping you?' she asked, her brain clearing. 'She jilts you, so you immediately get engaged to someone else, just to show her she's not the only pebble on the beach?'

Her heart twisted painfully. Was she right? Could he be that cruel? Would he use her like that, just to get his own back on the woman he loved? Buy her a flash engagement ring, make sure the whole world knew about it, then quietly break the whole thing off when the dust of Fiona's public jilting had settled?

'Well?' she demanded. 'No slick answer for once?' His bleak silence spurred her on to angry sarcasm. 'Or have you suddenly fallen madly in love with me? Somehow that would take a lot of swallowing!'

James glanced at the discreet face of his Rolex. He'd meant to spend the afternoon back in his apartment, going through a raft of paperwork. This was going to take longer than he'd thought.

'You sell yourself short, Mattie. You really should break the habit.' The words emerged on a breath of impatience, softened by slight amusement. 'And no,' he went on with no inflexion whatever, 'I have no more "fallen madly in love" with you than you have with me. In fact, I don't think the condition actually exists.'

He resigned himself to the loss of a full afternoon's useful work. He'd been over-optimistic when he'd imagined he could put his reasons for marriage in front of her in two minutes flat, and it would only take another three or four for her first-class brain to accept that the reasons and terms were both workable and desirable. Far from looking receptive, her face was screwed up in what could be nothing else but suppressed fury.

'All I ask is that you take time to listen to what I have to say. To kick off—' The sound of Edward letting himself in through the utility adjoining the kitchen made him bite his words off. Hell! He hadn't expected his partner back so soon. He'd scripted this as a rational, businesslike discussion, over in a few minutes, and it was rapidly turning into a farce.

His jawline grim, he narrow-eyed the older man as he walked into the room, blowing his fingers, his face ruddy from exercise in the bitingly cold air.

'So you decided to stay for lunch after all?' Edward hazarded. 'Thought you'd be well on your way by now. And, Mattie, if you're cooking, nothing for me. Getting a paunch.'

'Actually,' James drawled, thinking on his feet, mentally postponing that paperwork until later, much later, 'I'm taking Matts out to lunch, as a thank you for all the hard graft she's put in over the past few days.' His narrowed eyes impaled her with silver command. 'Go get your coat.'

Her instinct was to tell him not to dish out his orders in that brisk, authoritative voice, as if she were some lowly employee. Tell him to ask her nicely, and she'd think about it. But she'd controlled her emotions where James was concerned for more years than she cared to remember and she'd be a fool to give way to the need to snap and shout, indulge in a verbal stand-up fight.

He would simply turn his back on her, walk straight out, and she'd never discover what in damnation he'd been thinking about when he'd come out with that unbelievable proposal of marriage.

Besides, his eyes were positively glacial when he bit out, 'Scoot, Mattie. We don't have all day.'

The tone of his voice sent shivers down her spine. She had heard he was a force to be reckoned with, a man no one but an out-and-out fool would dare to cross, but in all the time she had known him she had never been afraid of him, or had the feeling that he was taking control of her life.

She went, almost tripping over her own feet, leaving the room before he could say or do anything else to add to her sense of angry confusion.

Of course she wasn't afraid of him, she told herself as she pulled Mrs Flax's overall over her head and searched in the hall cupboard for her serviceable waxed jacket. Afraid of what he was making her feel was more like it.

Disorientated. As if her brain had been put in a blender.

Stuffing her feet into leather boots, she tucked the bottoms of her trousers in with shaky fingers and James, dangling car keys, asked 'Ready?' making her jump out of her skin.

Impatient, she thought, glancing up at his tight jawline, the thin line of his mouth. And not the impatience of a man desperate to get his woman to himself. He'd been very quick to respond to her sarcastic question—of course he hadn't fallen in love with her. Any more than she'd fallen in love with him, he'd added.

If only he knew!

'Yes, I'm ready. And curious to know what this is all about,' she answered steadily enough, even though her heart was jittering about like a flying beetle trying to get out of a paper bag.

'I'll tell you over lunch.' And he'd throw in a bottle of wine. He wouldn't be drinking because he'd be driving later, but she looked as if she needed something to help her relax. She'd pulled a black woolly hat on her head, her bunched-back hair making it sit at an odd angle, the unflattering colour emphasising the pallor of her face. Poor little scrap!

He'd had this idea, had carefully examined it, found it to be sound and, as always, intended to act on it. Right now. No messing about. But she hadn't a clue what was in his head. He couldn't blame her for looking as if the world had gone insane around her.

'Let's go,' he said gently.

They drove half a mile to the village pub. Not far, the journey didn't give her nearly enough time to get her head together. James actually did want to marry her. He'd said so, but she was having difficulty taking it in.

Years ago, before she'd learned to control a tendency to indulge in foolish daydreams, she'd imagined him proposing. Down on one knee, moonlight and roses and all that stuff, vowing he'd always loved her, had been waiting for her to grow up.

Reality was totally different from the daydreams of a teenager. Wasn't it just!

The slack period between Christmas and the New Year celebrations meant they had the tiny, heavily beamed restaurant to themselves. The fire in the inglenook had only just been lit and the room was chilly. Mattie kept her bulky jacket on, but James plucked the woolly hat from her head as she scanned the short menu.

'That's better,' he said and she glanced across the table and caught the smile that softened the sculpted hardness of his mouth. He looked in full, complacent control. Suddenly, she wanted to slap him.

She laid the menu down. 'I'm not hungry. I just want you to tell me what's behind your singularly unromantic proposal of marriage.'

The clipped tone of her voice told him she was firing on all cylinders again. So right, his suggestion of marriage had confused her, but she was dealing with it. It was one of the things he admired about her—her ability to look at a problem from all angles and, eventually, to solve it, be it learning to drive or cooking a three-course meal.

'Over lunch, like civilised people. Choose something light if you haven't much appetite. I'm going for the lasagne.'

Civilised? Well, she supposed she could manage that. Just. She opted for an open prawn sandwich and drank a glass of the red wine he'd ordered while they waited. Her stomach closed up entirely when she saw the sheer size and bulk of her supposedly simple sandwich.

Gulping down more wine, she nibbled at a prawn. One down, five thousand more to go. How could he attack his loaded plate with such gusto? Easy. His stomach wasn't full of jitterbugging butterflies; his heart wasn't racked with painful contractions; he was completely unaffected.

She laid down her fork. 'I warn you, James, if, as I suspect, you want to get engaged in such a hurry to pay Fiona back, then you can forget it as far as I'm concerned. Find someone else to play games with.'

'Right.' He laid his fork down on his almost empty plate and leaned back, his eyes pinning her to her seat. 'I don't recall mentioning an engagement. What would be the point when we could be married within three weeks? And let's leave Fiona out of it.'

'We can't do that.' He was everything she'd ever wanted, but she wouldn't let herself be used. She wouldn't let herself in for that much pain. Living with him as his wife, knowing that every time he made love to her he would be pretending she was Fiona.

Her voice thick in her throat, she reminded him, 'You called being in love a "condition" and said you didn't think it existed. You've been dating gorgeous women for almost as long as I can remember, but it took Fiona to make you want to settle down and marry. You must love her.' Instinctively her voice lowered, softened with compassion; she didn't want to rub his nose in his hurt but it had to be done. 'I can imagine your pain when she rejected you, but jumping into marriage with someone else won't make it go away.'

She wanted to reach out and take his hand, comfort him, but he looked so formidably detached she didn't quite dare. She drained her wineglass recklessly.

'When you got over the Fiona thing and came to your senses, you'd find yourself saddled with a wife you couldn't love. And I wouldn't want to go through life knowing I was a poor second best.'

'You're not cut out to be an agony aunt, you don't know what you're talking about.' With difficulty he controlled his annoyance. She was thinking along the lines of a normal marriage, and that wasn't what he had in mind at all. And if she'd stop talking about Fiona for five seconds he'd put her in the picture.

He refilled her wineglass, sat back, and told her as much as her harping on about his broken engagement had made necessary. 'I took a look at my lifestyle and decided I needed a wife. Fiona was eminently suitable, beautiful to look at—' no need to mention her inventiveness in bed, that was his business '—a highly accomplished hostess. Essential, because, as you know, along with my home I inherited Mrs Briggs from my father. She's getting near retirement and is fine as far as the day-to-day running of the household goes, but ask her to organise a dinner party for half a dozen visiting businessmen who we're pitching a project to—plus their wives—and she's completely at sea. Well, you must have some idea what I'm talking about. So marriage seemed to be the answer. But it didn't work out. So, OK, the experience has probably soured me, put me off the man/woman bit, which is why, Mattie, what I'm proposing is what is loosely termed a marriage of convenience. In name only, that goes without saying.'

She was sure the smile he gave her was meant to be reassuring but the ache inside her intensified and the tiny spark of hope finally flickered out. Loving this man, she'd harboured the small but unquenchable hope that if she agreed to marry him then he might, in time, grow to love her. Regardless of the highly probable self-destructive outcome.

Stupid!

Rapidly gathering her considerable mental resources, she gave him a cool smile. 'You could hire someone—a good catering company, for instance—to organise sophisticated dinner parties at the drop of a hat. And I'm sure you could get one or other of the lovely young things you seem to attract like bees to a honeypot to act as hostess. You don't need a wife.'

'A wife would act as a deterrent, Mattie,' he said with a thin smile. 'Keep the swarms away from the honeypot. I'm no longer interested,' he added tiredly.

That figured, she thought, melting. He was still in love with Fiona and her rejection had hit him hard. Doubly hard, since it had to be a first. And he did look weary. There were shadows beneath his eyes and taut lines at the sides of his mouth. She wanted to take his hurt away, and knew she couldn't.

Instead she told him briskly, 'I can understand why you feel that way at the moment. But, believe me, it won't last. Women throw themselves at you, and eventually you'll be tempted. You're a sexy man, James Carter.'

He blinked at her and swallowed hard. Tried not to smile. She almost sounded as if she knew what she was talking about. What did she know about the lusts of the flesh? Zilch.

'Mattie, if we marry, I promise you I won't play around. You have my word on that.' It couldn't have been an easier promise to make. Sexual relationships were more trouble than they were worth. A jaded opinion, granted, but one he would firmly stick with.

His word. Once given, he never went back on it, she knew that. So if they married she wouldn't have to wonder where he was and who he was with if he didn't come home at night. Not that she had the slightest intention of accepting his proposal.

It was unthinkable.

Slurping more wine, she pointed out, 'You haven't thought this out. You're going to want children.'

He poured the last of the wine into her empty glass. She wanted chapter and verse, so he'd give it to her. He was beginning to enjoy this verbal fencing match. 'I was ten years old when I realised that I was just a nuisance as far as my parents were concerned. I demanded things of them they were unable to give. Time, consideration, thought. Love. I was sent away to school and it was a case of out of sight, out of mind. During the holidays there was the hired help to see that I was adequately fed. If I had worries, problems, triumphs—whatever—my parents didn't want to know. So no, I don't want children. I wouldn't be sure I could commit myself as thoroughly as a child deserves. My parents couldn't bring themselves to be interested in their offspring and the laws of nature mean I've inherited their genes.' He sketched a shrug. 'I wouldn't want to risk it.'

'Oh!' It was all Mattie could say. She wanted to throttle his parents but she couldn't because they were both dead. Killed years ago when the light aircraft they had been in had crashed into an Italian Alp. And she wanted to tell him that she would love any child of his like the most precious thing on earth, but she couldn't. Wanted to tell him that she could give him all the love and devotion his heartless parents had denied him. If he wanted it. But he didn't.

So she couldn't do that, either. She said, her voice very soft, 'I never knew that. About your unhappy childhood.' It went a long way towards explaining his aura of detachment, the untouchable quality that made him seem so in control of the events and people that surrounded him. 'You and your parents always seemed to get along together.'

'When we were together, which wasn't often, we were polite,' he conceded. 'I adapted as a child and learned not to wear my heart on my sleeve.' His dark brows drew together as he glanced at his watch. 'However, this isn't about me, I'm merely explaining why I don't have any desire to father children.'

'And Fiona was happy with that?' He didn't like her talking about his ex-fiancée. Well, he wouldn't, would he? But the wine had made her reckless, reckless enough to make an astute guess. 'I don't suppose she wanted to spoil her fabulous figure, or get baby dribble on her best Lacroix!' She batted back incipient tears. He hadn't asked if *she* wanted children, if *she* would be happy in such a sterile relationship. In fact, he wasn't considering her feelings at all. He probably thought she didn't have any.

'What would I get out of your proposed arrangement—except the stress of having to arrange dinner parties?' she demanded gruffly, beginning to regret her unprecedented intake of alcohol. Any minute now she would start to get over-emotional, blurt out things that would reveal her true feelings for him. Already there was a lump the size of a small house in her throat.

'Mattie—' he leaned closer, his forearms on the

table, his eyes warmer now. '—believe me, I've given this a whole lot of thought. It would be a satisfactory arrangement for both of us. Forget the social entertaining side of it—you're bright enough to get the hang of it, do anything you want to do. We get along well together, always have. I've enormous respect for your intelligence, your capacity for hard work. You're no raver, you won't play games or take me for a sucker—you've too much integrity. You're comfortable to be around. You're very soothing company. We'd make a good team. As for what you would gain from such an arrangement—' he smiled expansively, dazzling her, making her breath shudder in her lungs '—you get my name, my protection, my assurance that the demands of your work will always come before your duty as my wife—I know how much it means to you. You get a good home in one of the more sought-after areas of London.'

'You make me sound like a stray dog that needs to be taken in!' she spluttered, glad to stop puzzling over the compliments that had come over as not being complimentary at all and made her sound inexpressively dull.

James smothered a sigh. 'You're nearer the truth than you imagine. Your father might not have told you yet, but he's all set to sell up and move to an apartment in town. Taking Mrs Flax. And he's already making substantial noises about handing his shares in the business over to you, going into full retirement. If we marry, you have a home to go to and the business stays in the family.'

She was smart enough to see the sound common sense of that, but she was looking more poleaxed than ever. He tugged in a slow breath and asked gently, 'What do you see as the problems from your side? Face it, Matts, you're twenty-five years old and as far as I'm aware you've never been in a relationship. If your ambitions had run along the lines of a husband and family you'd have done something about it before now. Got out more, shown an interest in what you wore. Done the things a woman does—you know, hairstyles and make-up. That being said, where's the harm in two people who like and respect each other teaming up and forming a successful partnership?'

Mattie stared at him, her eyes wide and unfocussed. She felt as if the bottom had dropped right out of her life and suddenly marriage to James seemed a rock she could cling to. Forget his astute reasoning behind his desire to control her father's fifty-per-cent holding in the company, forget that he didn't love her, and never could. She could handle that; she'd had plenty of practice over the last decade.

What she couldn't handle was this sense of betrayal. She had believed that her father, at least, saw her worth, valued her. But he hadn't bothered to consult her over his decision to sell the family home, hand over his business shares.

It really hurt.

Early on in her life she'd realised she was a disappointment to her mother. Straight, lank hair, plain little face, skinny body. Nothing her mother could do made her pretty—she'd told her so often enough. When her beautiful baby brother had been born her mother had as good as forgotten she'd existed. And when he'd died from meningitis she had gone to pieces, had never recovered, shutting both her daughter and her husband out until, eventually, she'd left them.

But she, Mattie, had discovered how to make her father proud of her. Good grades at school. Not only good, the best. She'd learned to keep her head down, keep at her studies, make the best get better.

But he couldn't have been proud of her, rated her very highly. If he'd thought anything of her he would have discussed such life-changing decisions with her first. Wouldn't he?

She stood up unsteadily, the sight of her barely touched meal, the dregs of wine in her glass, making her feel slightly nauseous.

'I'll marry you, James. Just let me know the date and venue and I'll be there.'

CHAPTER THREE

MATTIE stuck her hands in the pockets of her jacket—quilted amber silk; Armani, no less—and shivered. More from apprehension than the darkly bitter January evening air.

What would her father think of the way she was dolled up?

She shot an aggravated glance up at the monitor over the windy platform. His train was late. After a week in London, on some unspecified business or other, he'd phoned last night and asked her, in Mrs Flax's absence, to meet his train.

The drive into Lewes had been a nightmare. She loathed driving at night; it made her more than nervous. Oncoming headlights always blinded her and when she scrabbled around for her own dip switch she usually managed to activate her wipers instead or, even worse, indicate a turn she had no intention of making.

To add to her jitters she'd been agonising over what her father would make of her new image. Someone unsuccessfully trying to make a silk purse out of a sow's ear? Pitiful, perhaps? Tarty? Oh, heaven forbid! Or simply and shamingly hilarious?

Not that her father's reaction would trouble her overmuch, of course, but it would give her a good indication of what James would think.

And all of it was Dawn's fault!

She'd arrived in the middle of last week, pounding

on the front door as if the Mafia were after her. 'I've taken a few days off to help you out, Matts. We've got to get you sorted! Ten days until the wedding and I bet you haven't given a single thought to what you're going to wear! Where's your father?'

'In town for a week.'

'Good. That's where we're heading and if he's away we won't have to waste time explaining what we're doing—or, knowing you, asking for his permission! All you have to do is grab your credit cards and lock the doors.'

'You're mad!'

'No. Fairy godmother or angel of mercy. Either will do me so take your pick. You're going to get a make-over, and you're going to like it. And even if you don't, I'm pretty sure James will.'

No, he wouldn't. Mattie's thoughts were mutinous. He picked me because I'm comfortable, soothing, not a raver. A mouse.

'He proposed to me as I am,' she pointed out tartly. 'Warts and all.'

'And full marks for playing your cards right! I told you to, remember?' Dawn grinned back at her. 'But your transformation will be the icing on the cake as far as he's concerned. Haven't I always told you you could be really gorgeous if you put your mind to it and stopped dressing like your own grandmother? Now I'm going to prove myself right.'

A vivid flash of memory. Her mother buttoning her into yet another frilly dress, tying ribbons in her hair. Sitting back on her heels surveying the unpromising result with an exasperated frown. 'I don't know why I bother—stand up straight, child, and stop scowling! Why can't you be more like your little

friend, Dawn? I don't know where you got your plain
looks from—certainly not from my side of the family!'

For the very first time a stab of defiance had gone
through her. What if she were to prove her mother's
opinion of her irredeemable plainness wrong? Could
she? Maybe with her best friend's advice on clothes
that might actually suit her instead of merely keeping
her decently covered she could look a little more
interesting?

But the three days they'd spent in London had left
her with very mixed emotions. Arriving home late
yesterday evening with what seemed like a trailer-
load of exclusive carrierbags, a bucketful of cosmet-
ics, seventy-five per cent less hair and a severe hole
in her current account, she'd begun to have serious
doubts.

Without her friend's enthusiasm, energy and sheer
pushing power she was beginning to doubt the wisdom of the exercise.

True, her hair felt better for being styled into a
sleek, jaw-length bob. It looked better, too. Shinier,
the colour a richer shade of chestnut. But the clothes
she'd been dragooned into buying—she wasn't too
sure about them; not sure at all, if she was honest.

She didn't feel like herself any more. James
wanted a quiet, unobtrusive wife to cope with the
business entertaining he had to do, to stop other
women making a play for him because after the
Fiona fiasco he was off the lot of them. Would he
call the whole thing off when he saw her like this
because a tarty-looking wife was not what he
wanted?

She glanced down at the narrow, butter-soft,

cream-coloured leather trousers, the high-heeled ankle boots that admittedly made her legs look longer and more elegant than they really were, and shivered.

And if he did call the wedding off, would that be such a bad thing? The thought edged its way into her brain and stuck there.

She'd probably overreacted to the way her father had neglected to give her even a tiny hint of his far-reaching future plans, she thought with a miserable flash of insight. She'd put her whole future happiness on the line when she'd agreed to such a sterile relationship with a man who could never love her.

It wouldn't have been nearly as bad if she couldn't love him, either. But she could. And did.

When the train finally arrived she scanned the alighting passengers, chewing on the corner of her lower lip, saw her father and straightened her shoulders. He would have walked straight past her until she touched his arm and said with unprecedented sharpness, 'You could have used your mobile and warned me your train was running an hour late. And unless you want to end up as an accident statistic you can drive home.'

She'd been brooding over his insulting secrecy, the way he hadn't bothered to so much as mention his future plans to her, not even when she and James had told him of their marriage, and her annoyance spiked her voice. But Edward Trent didn't comment on her less than welcoming greeting.

His eyes widened. 'Mattie? Good Lord, I didn't recognise you—what have you done to yourself?'

Which didn't augur well. What if James' reaction was the same? Incredulous shock!

He scrutinised her under the platform lights. 'It's

not like you to wear bright colours—you look like a stranger! And you didn't get that fancy outfit in one of the local shops.'

'Dawn and I went up to London for a day or so,' she responded stiffly. He was grinning now. Actually grinning. Did she look that funny? She must do. He never commented on what she was wearing and he certainly didn't burst into laughter at her appearance.

'I might have known she'd be behind it.' He chuckled. 'She's always been a flashy dresser. Pretty with it, mind. By the way, like the way you've done your hair. Cut some of it off, have you?' He started to walk. 'Let's get a move on. Damned cold, standing here.'

'Tell me about it!' Mattie muttered, following. So it was all right to wear bright clothes, but only if you were pretty! And she most certainly wasn't!

The fragile confidence in her new appearance, brought to tenuous life by Dawn's insistence on her visiting a top hair stylist, learning how to apply make-up properly, choosing the designer labels that her friend vowed suited her so well, had never been strong and was rapidly ebbing away completely.

Thankfully, her father was only too happy to take her ignition keys. He didn't rate her driving skills any more than James did. She settled herself into the passenger seat and sank into her dreary thoughts.

The jaunt to London had been an expensive waste. She should never have let Dawn talk her into trying to turn herself into something she wasn't. The only sensible thing to do was push the new clothes she'd splurged out on into the very back of her wardrobe and go back to wearing the plain, serviceable things she was used to and felt comfortable in.

And the second sensible thing to do was phone James. Tonight. Explain that she'd reconsidered, call the wedding off.

It was the only course of action to take, she told herself sternly when the car finally swept up the driveway to Berrington House. She couldn't imagine what had made her accept his cold-blooded proposal in the first place.

But she could. Of course she could, she reminded herself as she stood in the hallway waiting for her father to garage her car. When her father had taken James into his confidence, told him he was thinking of taking full retirement, of selling the family home and moving into an apartment with Mrs Flax to look after him, he had overlooked her entirely, just as if she didn't even exist.

It had felt like abandonment. Brought back the feelings of betrayal and inadequacy she'd experienced when her mother had walked out all those years ago, never to get in touch again, or remember her birthdays, or even ask how she was.

It had made marriage to James, even a marriage that would be no marriage at all, seem like a haven of security.

She was going to have no part of it.

She could stand on her own, make a life for herself. She could travel, take up private tutoring. With her qualifications she could easily find employment teaching English to Spanish children—or French, German or Italian. She wasn't the hopelessly vague and impractical creature everyone seemed to think she was.

'I think you have something to tell me,' she stated as her father closed the door behind him, dropped his light leather suitcase on the floor and began to unbutton his overcoat.

'I have?'

'I think so.' They were going to have this out before she phoned James to tell him she wouldn't marry him. Tonight she was going to take the initiative for probably the first time in her life, even if the thought of turning James down did make her feel weak and tearful. 'Retirement, handing over the shares in the business to me, an apartment in town for you and Mrs Flax. Does that jog your memory?'

'Ah.' He had the grace to look uncomfortable. 'So James told you. I would have told you—'

'When?' she broke in. 'When the new owners moved in here and you finally remembered I existed, couldn't really be left behind like a piece of unwanted furniture they could either make use of, or throw on the nearest skip?'

If possible, he looked more incredulous than he had at the station when confronted by her new appearance. He wasn't used to her standing up for herself.

'Nothing like that!' he answered gruffly. 'Look, let's go through and make cocoa. I fancy an early night, and while we drink it I'll explain everything.'

Tight-lipped, Mattie led the way to the kitchen and took a bottle of the white wine left over from Christmas out of the fridge and busied herself with the corkscrew. She felt in need of something stronger than the ritualistic bedtime mug of cocoa.

Apart from raising one bushy eyebrow, Edward said nothing, just set about making his own hot drink, and when that was done he found his daughter looking at him almost aggressively over the rim of her glass.

'Sit down, Mattie. You weren't meant to feel left out of my plans.'

'Then why was I?' she returned, but less sharply. He really did look tired, she thought with a pang, and she normally didn't have a confrontational bone in her body.

She did as he'd suggested and joined him at the table, cradling the bowl of her wineglass in her small, long-fingered hands. 'Have you reached a firm decision about moving?' she asked, determined to cool down for his sake.

'Yes,' he acknowledged. 'But only forty-eight hours ago when I found the ideal apartment. Since my GP advised me to take things more easily—no, it's nothing to worry about,' he said quickly, seeing the sudden flare of anxiety in her eyes. 'Problems with blood pressure, nothing that can't be sorted. But it did start me thinking. James is more than capable of running the business without my input. And I could sell out to him, but I'd rather the shares went to you, stayed in the family.

'Naturally, I discussed the possibility with him. And this barn of a place—' he spread his hands expressively '—the three of us have rattled around here for too long. I sounded Mrs Flax—Emily—out. I said nothing definite, of course. An apartment in London would be easier for her to cope with. Close to the things that make life more agreeable. Emily and I share several interests—light opera, the theatre, visiting museums, Italian restaurants, that sort of thing. And more of a social life for you, I thought. You spend too much time alone here.

'And then you and James dropped your marriage bombshell and you were out of the frame where my plans were concerned. What had been vague ideas became a little more solid then. So I spent the week in London. Apartment hunting, meetings with the company solicitor arranging for my shares to be transferred to your name. And I hadn't mentioned any of this to you.'

His eyes smiled at her. 'Not because I'd overlooked you, but because nothing was definite, not at that stage. You're not the most practical person I know, happiest when shut away with your work. I didn't want you getting into a flap until I'd really decided that the move, if I were to make it, would work.'

'You thought I'd run around like a headless chicken,' Mattie commented wryly. It seemed that everyone had an unflattering opinion of her. And no doubt she had earned it. Well, she thought robustly, things were going to change. She was going to change.

She swallowed her wine and poured herself another glass, opened her mouth to tell her father that her marriage to James was off, then closed it again as something inside her tightened into a painful knot.

James himself had to be the first to know of her decision; she owed him that much. She asked instead, 'So did you find a suitable apartment for you—and Emily?'

Was there more to this than met the eye? Mrs Flax had been with them for years, since Mattie's mother had gone to pieces after the death of her idolised baby son. A year or two younger than Mattie's father, the widowed Emily Flax was a capable, still handsome woman, kindly and caring. It would be wonderful if they married. Her father deserved to be happy after the dark years of loneliness.

'Yes. About a ten-minute walk from James' house in Belgravia, so we'll be able to see a lot of each other after you're married. Did you see much of James while you and Dawn were in London?'

'No.'

Nothing. As far as she knew he had no idea she'd been away from Berrington for the past few days. Though he might have phoned. She'd check the answer machine for messages before she got in touch with him. The only contact she'd had with him since she'd agreed to marry him had been his calls to keep her up to date with the arrangement he was making: a simple civil ceremony, no fuss, no honeymoon because in the circumstances there was no point— which was unflattering but completely understandable when they both knew their marriage wouldn't be a real one, she thought, her heart aching.

Her father, on the point of rising, sank back in his seat, a frown pulling his brows together. 'I can't pretend I wasn't delighted when James told me you were to marry. I guess every father wants to hand the safe keeping and happiness of his daughter over to a man he can trust implicitly. But until recently he was engaged to that awful woman. You must have discussed it, of course. But are you sure he can make you happy?'

He could, if he loved her. He could make her the happiest, most ecstatic woman on the planet. But he didn't. And wearing his wedding ring would make her unspeakably miserable, she knew that now. But time enough to tell her father the whole thing was off in the morning, after she'd phoned James.

'Let me worry about that,' she evaded, taking his empty cocoa mug over to the sink. 'Why don't you turn in? You did say you needed an early night. It's gone ten o'clock already.'

And she needed time to mentally reinforce her decision to phone James and tell him she couldn't marry him, explain that it would be wrong for both of them. Despite what he'd said, he was a normal male, with all the needs that implied. Sooner or later he'd face a temptation he would find almost impossible to resist, he'd meet some gorgeous woman who would make him forget he'd said he wouldn't stray, make a mockery of his cynical statement that he was off the whole idea of sex.

And if he succumbed to that type of temptation he'd be riddled with guilt because he'd made a promise to her, one that was impossible to keep, and he would suffer because he was an honourable man. And she would suffer, too. Unbearably.

She barely heard her father's goodnight and only realised she was alone when the silence tortured her nerve-endings. Time to bite the bullet, to quash the foolish, flickering hope that, given time, he could learn to love her, that their marriage could become a real one.

It simply wasn't going to happen.

Passing through the hall on her way to the study, she slid the silk-covered buttons of her jacket from their moorings and shrugged out of it. The thought of what she was going to have to say to James was making her overheat. She'd be throwing away something so very precious.

Her throat closed up, everything inside her tightening. It was as if she were going to the dentist for a particularly gruelling session of deep-root fillings! Only worse.

She turned to head for the study and the phone but the sound of the main door opening had her swinging back, the sound of James' voice startling her violently.

'So you *are* here. I was worried; you didn't answer my calls, Mattie—'

His voice faded. Mattie stared at him. Framed by the blackness of the night beyond the open doorway, he looked mysterious, dangerous and compellingly gorgeous. How could she tell him she wouldn't marry him when she wanted him, adored him, with every atom of her being?

Yet she must. She knew she must.

He was staring back at her, his slightly hooded silver eyes sliding down from her face, covering the pert, rounded breasts revealed by the skinny-rib V-necked top that matched the discarded jacket, taking in the flatness of her tiny waist, the slight flare of hips and slenderness of thigh covered in creamy-looking leather.

He was looking at her as if he'd never seen her before, as if what he saw mesmerised him. As if he really and truly enjoyed what he was seeing. It was obvious from his riveted expression that he didn't find the transformation shocking, pathetic or funny!

For the first time he was seeing her as a real woman. A desirable woman?

Certainty blossomed fiercely in Mattie's heart. Fiercely and intoxicatingly sweetly. Her good intentions disappeared into the dark winter night. She wasn't going to quit on him. Oh, however could she have harboured such a defeatist thought? The slide of his eyes over her body was like the physical touch of a lover; it made her flesh tingle, made her heart swell with yearning.

Sexual interest—the dawning of awareness of her on his part—was something solid and hopeful to work on. Perhaps, given time, he could fall in love with her.

Without taking his eyes off her, James pushed the door back into its frame, shutting out the night. Mattie, dressed as she was, without the shapeless, dowdy things she normally went around in, was a shattering revelation. Five-two of slender, seductively curving perfection. All woman, and then some.

The niggling anxieties that had brought him dutifully down here tonight hardened into something very much sharper than concern over the well being of a fellow human, something he couldn't put a name to.

'So where were you?' His voice sounded harsh and accusing to his own ears, but he couldn't help that. She hadn't returned a single one of his calls over the last few days, and she obviously hadn't come down with a bad dose of flu or fallen down the stairs and been lying around with a broken limb because she couldn't get to a phone and there'd been no one home to help her. By the look of her she'd been out, strutting her stuff while her father and the housekeeper had both been away.

Yes! Mattie resisted the impulse to punch the air. He sounded like a suspicious husband—jealous, even!

She gave him a slow smile, lowering her lashes.

James came closer, sucking in his breath. 'I left messages but you didn't bother to return them. When I got back this evening from a site visit in York I phoned again. Still no answer. I drove down because I was worried. So where were you?'

That smile, dammit, made his blood pressure rise angrily. The subtle, bronzy tones of that apparently expertly applied lipstick made her even, pretty teeth almost impossibly white and her generous mouth definitely sultry.

Hell, she never wore the stuff as far as he knew. Just the lightest smudge of pale pink if she was going out somewhere she deemed merited the effort.

He was more than annoyed with her, Mattie thought. He was spitting mad! Never before, in all the time she'd known him, had he displayed any emotion other than mild brotherly affection—or a rather patronising amusement—where she was concerned.

She was getting there!

'Your call this evening must have coincided with my driving to Lewes to meet Dad's train,' she said soothingly. 'And before that, Dawn and I were in London, shopping for my trousseau.' And thank heaven she'd been too busy getting herself hot and bothered about her new image to even think of listening for messages during the twenty-four hours she'd been back here, she thought elatedly.

If she had done so, this evening as she'd intended she would have returned his calls and told him the wedding was cancelled.

The close brush with might-have-been made her voice breathless as she said, 'I'm sorry you were worried; as you can see, there was no need. But it was thoughtful of you to go to the trouble to check up on me. Now come on through to the kitchen. I'll fix you some supper and you can sleep over. You won't want to drive back to town tonight.'

Something was fizzing through her veins. Sheer, gut-twisting excitement, the certainty that—thanks to Dawn's pestering—James was seeing her as a real flesh-and-blood woman for the first time ever, that there was something here she could build on if only she could be patient, or clever, enough. Whatever, for possibly the first time in her life she felt gloriously liberated, invulnerable.

Ungritting his teeth, James followed, his eyes annoyingly glued to her neat little backside so lovingly covered by butter-soft leather.

When, and how, had his old friend Matts changed from a quiet, mouse-like, studious, vague and innocently sexless creature into a woman who would make any red-blooded male suddenly overdose on testosterone?

The comfortable, undemanding paper marriage he'd proposed was going to take some honouring. But it was what she'd agreed to, what she was expecting, and if he wasn't prepared to call the whole thing off, then that was the way it was going to have to be.

Shouldn't be too difficult, though, he glumly assured himself as he sat at the kitchen table, tossed back the whisky she'd given him and watched her beat eggs for the omelette she'd offered to make.

Given that he'd decided that women, the whole pack of them, weren't worth bothering with, it shouldn't be difficult at all.

Besides, that friend of hers had probably bullied

her into wearing something that actually revealed the hitherto unguessed-at fact that she had a beautiful body, small but perfectly proportioned, and forced her into shopping for a so-called trousseau. And Mattie would have gone along with it because she would have had little option, because no one but they knew that this forthcoming marriage was one of mutual convenience, a total sham.

Once she was settled into his home—and he'd already told her she could choose any room she liked as her private work space—she would revert to being herself. Without the pressure coming from Dawn, who obviously thought a wedding in the offing was an excuse to get dolled up to the nines, good old Matts would bury her nose in her work and bury her body in the shapeless, mud-coloured things that comprised her normal wardrobe.

The status quo would be restored, and that he could handle. No problem.

No problem at all.

CHAPTER FOUR

'THE way we conduct our marriage is no one's business but our own,' James stated as repressively as he could manage through throat muscles that were becoming so restricted they were in danger of seizing up completely.

'Yes, I do know that.' Mattie smiled sweetly, lifting the silver covers from the dishes on the heated trolley, the sleek wings of her hair brushing against her slightly flushed cheeks. 'But think about it, James. I'm sure Mrs Briggs is a treasure, and discreet, and very loyal—but she is only human. I managed to put her mind at rest over our separate bedrooms—I told her it was the modern way. She did look a bit bewildered but I think she swallowed it. Then you chose to spend all day at the office—the first day of our marriage—and I know she found that very odd. So what could I do?'

Again that smile, slanted in his direction. This time warmly conspiratorial. Her mouth was a glossy scarlet tonight. Lush. Made for kissing. James ran a finger beneath the pristine white linen collar of his shirt. Was the central heating way too high, or was he coming down with something? Like a bad case of lust?

'I said what a pity it was that something so important had come up, making it imperative that you tied yourself to your desk all day, asked her to pre-

pare dinner and then take the rest of the night off.
Then I made sure she saw me dressed like this.'

Like a walking invitation to get between the
sheets!

A diaphanous piece of black nonsense, tiny straps
that looked as if they would snap if touched sup-
porting a scooped-out top that clung to two pert and
perfect breasts, skimming a tiny waist to cling to de-
lectably curvy hips, ending in a fluttery hem just
above her knees.

Amazingly pretty knees.

He swallowed convulsively.

'So she believes we're now enjoying a romantic
dinner for two and are on no account to be dis-
turbed,' she said with a disarmingly husky giggle
which sent his blood pressure into orbit. 'Which
should put paid to any suspicions she might be har-
bouring about the state of our marriage. As I said,
she is only human, as prone to speculation and gossip
as the rest of us.'

She was transferring dishes from the trolley to the
table which had been laid in the velvet-curtained
window alcove. Gleaming mahogany set with silver,
crystal, a small vase of sweetly scented freesias, can-
dles—the whole caboodle.

She moved beautifully. Gracefully.

Had the sloughing of the smothering things she
normally wore liberated her body, freed it up, so to
speak? Or had her movements always been so elegant and he hadn't noticed?

'We don't want people gossiping about us and our
marriage, do we?' she asked him earnestly, pointing
out, 'It might suit us perfectly, but that's between the
two of us. If it became known, or even suspected,

that ours is a marriage in name only, you would have no protection whatsoever from the droves of females who throw themselves at you—which is what you wanted. And I don't want to be sneered at because I'm married to a man who doesn't fancy me in the least.'

Didn't fancy her? Was she winding him up? he thought irately. Did she dress and put on her make-up without looking in a mirror!

Dammit, what man wouldn't fancy her, take one look at her and imagine how it would be to slide those fragile straps from those creamy white shoulders, slip the filmy black fabric slowly away from those rounded breasts, dip his head to taste—?

Gritting his teeth, he forced his thoughts from that dangerous path, forced himself to look deep into her eyes, then slowly exhaled, reassured, deeply contrite for his initial unspoken flare of anger.

The golden irises were Mattie's, his Mattie's. Wide, trusting, innocent. No hint of teasing. Definitely no hint that she'd been winding him up. And she did have a point. Of course she wouldn't want to be a source of sniggering speculation. She didn't deserve that. And she almost certainly wasn't aware of the deplorable effect she was having on him.

And hadn't she just said that the type of marriage they'd entered into suited her perfectly?

'So let's eat,' he suggested lightly as he walked across his elegantly furnished drawing room to join her at the table where she was cradling an unopened bottle of wine on her exquisite bosom.

Somehow he was going to have to explain about the way men were. Delicately. That went without saying because, despite the way she looked, Mattie was still wet behind the ears in the matter of sexual behaviour.

'Would you open the wine? Somehow I always seem to make a mess of it.' She sounded strangely breathless, still clutching the bottle to her body, her gaze wide and ingenuous. James slanted one dark brow upwards, his mouth softening. She was still the vague, impractical Matts he had grown fond of over the years. How could he have imagined that she'd suddenly transmogrified into a siren?

'Of course.' He reached for the bottle. Big, big mistake. Inevitably, given the way she was clinging to the wretched thing, the backs of his fingers grazed the underswell of one exquisitely formed breast. The shock of feeling the firmness, the warmth of the lightly scented flesh through the insubstantial barrier of fabric, sent deep shudders rocketing through the length of his body.

Ye gods! If they were to stick to the sort of marriage that she herself had said, only minutes ago, suited her perfectly, then the lecture he was about to give her couldn't start soon enough.

His hands were still shaking as he drew the cork, his eyes drawn unwillingly to the grace of slender, naked arms as she ladled what looked like pheasant in a rich red wine sauce onto a plate, adding tiny wedges of crispy roast potatoes.

'Greens?' she asked, the small, long-fingered hand that held the silver server hovering over a dish of broccoli. A small smile played at the corners of her mouth.

He nodded curtly, pouring wine. Why had he never noticed the enchanting dimple at the side of her mouth? Because he'd never really looked at her before, he told himself wryly, just accepted the way she looked—at least, the way she used to look—as he would accept the shape, size and colour of an old piece of furniture that had been hanging about the place for years.

He had never seen her potential, never even thought about it. But Dawn had, drat the woman, leaving him with warning bells clanging in his brain, loud enough to permanently deafen him.

'Mrs Briggs is a wonderful cook,' Mattie said as they sat down. 'But, as you told me, she is slowing down. And I'm next to hopeless. So, as I see it, the best way to jump the hurdle of large-scale business entertaining, with almost no notice, is for me to suss out various catering establishments—the sort that work at the speed of light—and make arrangements with them. Mrs Briggs and I can manage the table settings, flowers and so on. I can't see there'd be any problem. Can you?'

'What?' James shook his head to clear the red mist from his eyes. He had barely heard a word she'd been saying, he'd been looking at the way the candlelight enhanced her, casting warm shadows over exposed flesh, deepening the mystery of her, glancing off those high cheek-bones, intensifying the pouty shape of her mouth.

'Sorry,' he muttered hoarsely. 'I'm sure you can work something out. And talking of work, when will you be starting your next project? Did you choose a room for your study?'

This he could handle. He metaphorically grasped the subject with both hands. With her work to engross her everything would return to normal. He was pretty damn sure it would. Out would go the fancy stuff she'd taken to wearing—the soft, lemon-yellow suit she'd worn to the civil ceremony of marriage yesterday and had been particularly fetching—and back would come the comfortable sludge of baggy sweaters, droopy skirts or shapeless old jeans that always seemed several sizes too large.

He'd be out of temptation's way. The temptation to discover her, know every delicious inch of her, find out for himself whether that ultra feminine body, those sensually full lips would live up to the promise that seemed to be exuding from every pore of her skin.

He shifted his chair closer to the table. Allowing his thoughts along that particular road was having the expected yet, under the circumstances, disastrous effect on a certain part of his anatomy.

But, 'No,' she said, laying down her cutlery. 'Mrs Briggs and I did carry my boxes of stuff up to one of the spare rooms, out of the way. And I've been in touch with the agency I use and told them I won't be taking on any more projects for a while. I want to be a proper wife to you, James.'

A proper wife! Did she know what she was saying?

The way she was looking at him through her lashes, dimpling slightly, would suggest so. He picked up his wineglass and drained it. He was getting overheated again, overreacting. Matts didn't have a seductive, teasing or wily bone in her body.

And she confirmed it. 'My job description as your wife includes acting as your hostess, arranging your social diary. Now I'm not used to that sort of thing, as you know. I've led a very quiet life. But I won't

let you down, I'll get my head around it. And for the
sake of appearances, I do think it would be politic
for us to be seen around together. Act the part of any
normal, newly-married couple. Not that this marriage
is normal,' she quickly assured him, 'but we don't
want everyone—and that means everyone who
knows about what happened with Fiona—to know it,
too. So we do need to spend a lot of time together.'
She gave him a soft, commiserating smile. 'Pud-
ding?'

'No. No, thank you.' He shook his head distract-
edly while she served herself a generous slice of bil-
berry tart, smothering it with fresh cream.

Spend a lot of time together? Wasn't that why he'd
gone into the office today—to put himself out of
reach of temptation?

The temptation to make love to his own wife!

The situation was getting farcical. It was time he
told her as it was.

'Matts—perhaps we should have some plain
speaking.' His voice sounded distinctly hoarse. He
cleared his throat. 'We both know what we want out
of this marriage. Comfortable companionship for
starters, nothing more, nothing less. The business
staying in the family, as it were. For you, a good
home, the freedom to pursue your career, to run my
home as you see fit without having to play second
fiddle and gooseberry to your father and Emily
Flax—I think we both know which way that particular wind's blowing, don't we? And for me, a wife
to deter the hordes of women on the make out there.
As I told you, quite frankly, I've had it up to here—'
he slashed a line across his throat '—with kiss-me-

quick, gold-digging harpies. Anything female under fifty, for that matter!'

'Oh.' she widened her eyes and laid down her spoon. 'I'm nowhere near fifty!'

'Of course not. But you're not female, either.'

'I'm not?' Thick lashes fluttered. The tip of a pretty pink tongue captured a speck of cream from the corner of her mouth.

James shuddered. Lord, was he ever making a pig's ear of this!

'What I meant was,' he said desperately, 'that I've never *thought* of you as being a female. Just Mattie, brainy and studious. Comfortable to be with and, unlike others of the female sex, totally undemanding of male time and attention. I mean—' he leaned his arms on the table, warming to the subject, needing to get his message through to her '—have you ever given me come-hither looks, asked me if the shade of lipstick you were wearing suited you? No, of course you haven't. Asked me if whatever it was you were wearing would look better without a bra? No, of course—' He choked off the words. Why the dickens had he used that example when it was perfectly obvious she wasn't wearing one?

He made a huge effort to pull himself together, to take control of a situation that was in danger of getting out of hand. 'Look, what I'm trying to say is I've always thought of you as a kid sister.'

'When you thought of me at all,' she came back snippily.

Sharp, that. He sucked a deep breath in between his teeth. Hell, no way did he want to hurt her feelings. And of course he'd thought of her. Often. As a little mouse, stuck in her ivory tower. Poring over

her books. As different from the brittle, glittery, ultra-sophisticated females who had drifted in and out
of his life as it was possible to be.

But anything less mouse-like than his newly-
wedded wife was hard to imagine! That was the crux
of the matter.

'Naturally, I've thought of you,' he assured her
quickly. 'After all, I've known you for ever. I
watched you grow up, applauded louder than anyone
when you got your degree, and earlier,' he reminded
her, because suddenly he couldn't bear it if she
thought that she'd never been more than a shadowy,
insignificant non-entity in the background of his
business partner's life, 'when the mother you hadn't
seen or heard of for years was killed on the streets
of Manchester by that joy-rider, my first thought after
going with your father to formally identify the body
was to comfort you. So, yes, Mattie, I have thought
of you.'

'You were very kind,' she said softly, her eyes
limpid. She remembered every word he'd said, the
way he'd folded her in his arms and comforted her.
She would never forget. It had been then that she had
fallen in love with him, the infatuation that had been
her secret for the past two years changing into something so much deeper, so very permanent.

'Yes, well,' he said gruffly, 'I'm not asking for
plaudits, just reminding you that I have thought of
you. As a sister, almost, like I said.' He dragged in
a breath. It was important to stress that aspect of their
relationship. Now this was the tricky part. 'Not in a
sexual way at all. We both knew what we wanted
from this marriage, and sex definitely wasn't a part
of it.'

Liar, he derided himself. What he most wanted, right now, was to take her to bed. But that would be a monumental mistake, and bad news for her because it wasn't what she wanted, either. She would never have agreed to a paper marriage if she'd had any feelings for him in that direction.

'Sex muddies things,' he told her. 'It gets in the way. It might be great while it lasts. But it doesn't. Last, I mean. And neither of us wants that kind of messy complication in what could otherwise be a mutually advantageous partnership.'

He pushed his chair back from the table and levered himself to his feet. Beginning to sweat now. But he made sure he sounded kind, slightly amused, even, when he told her, 'However, I am a fully functional male, and the way you've taken to dressing recently could lead to the type of complications neither of us wants. For our mutual peace of mind I suggest you dress as you used to. I'm sure you understand what I mean.'

Hell—he was coming over as a pompous, patronising nerd. And perhaps he'd put the whole thing badly. But it was said now and he needed to get out of here. Needed a cold shower. He hadn't felt so out of control, so much at the mercy of his hormones since he'd been a randy teenager!

'I'll say goodnight,' he muttered hoarsely and raced for the door.

Mattie stepped out of the little black slip dress Dawn had insisted was perfect for her and hung it carefully back in the wardrobe with all the other goodies.

If James had his way, she would never wear any of them. Part of her agreed with him. What she was doing was scary. And, if she were to be cruelly honest with herself, decidedly sneaky!

What was it Dawn had said? 'What have you got to lose? Nothing. So go for it, girl, pull out all the stops. I told you you'd be gorgeous if you made the effort. And if James has seen you as the knock-out you really are, and you're married, living together, then it doesn't take a genius to know that sooner or later you'll end up doing what comes naturally!'

Mattie sighed. It came right up from her toes. Dawn had said she had nothing to lose. But she had. She could lose his friendship, his respect. And she didn't want him driven to the point of having sex with her—which was what the poor love had been warning her of over dinner tonight. She wanted him to fall in love with her, and that was very different.

An impossible mountain to climb. Hadn't he told her, when he'd first proposed, that he didn't believe in the condition?

Jumpy as a kitten on a bed of thistles, Mattie opted for a long soak in the bath instead of her usual quick shower. But it did nothing to relax her and she resigned herself to an uneasy night as she pulled her voluminous cotton nightie over her head, craving the comfort of the familiar and refusing, absolutely refusing, to put herself in any of the slinky satin and lace things that Dawn had insisted were *de rigueur* for a new bride.

Dawn. Had she made a huge mistake when she'd taken her old friend fully into her confidence, swearing her to absolute secrecy?

That night, only just over a week ago, she'd been convinced that the only sane thing to do was to tell James she couldn't marry him. But the look of totally unprecedented, blatant male appreciation in his eyes had put her on such a high that she'd done no such thing, as certain as she could possibly have been that, given time, their marriage could become a real one. That, for him, love could grow from such a beginning.

The following morning her mood had swung the other way entirely, helped by the fact that he must have left well before she'd come downstairs to make him breakfast. Just a note in his bold, distinctive hand, left on the kitchen table: "Matts, pack all the gear you don't need for the coming week. I'll send someone round to pick it up on Wednesday and transfer it to Belgravia. Speak to you soon."

He hadn't even hung around long enough to say good morning! His interest in her went no further than the convenience of having a quiet, unobtrusive wife in the background to ward off female predators.

If the gorgeous creatures who had sashayed through his life with monotonous regularity—culminating in the top-drawer Fiona Campbell-Blair—hadn't been able to win his love, what hope did she have?

The look she'd seen in his eyes the night before had not been appreciation; how could it have been? Surprise that she was actually wearing something that fitted her, was colourful and suited her for once in her life was much nearer the mark.

Confused, not knowing which way to jump, she'd phoned Dawn and told all. Only to receive the advice she was now acting on.

Bad advice, she thought mournfully. She shouldn't have listened. When she'd finally come to her senses she should have acted on what her own brain was telling her, not gone whining to Dawn whose eternal optimism bordered on the insane!

She should have extricated herself from this mess when she'd had the opportunity, not allowed herself to hope, because hope was getting her nowhere, just earning herself a warning-off from a man who didn't want to find himself wanting sex with her!

Sex wasn't what she wanted, either. Well, she did—of course she did. With him. He was the only man who had ever made her feel like this. But not sex without love, because it would be meaningless— demeaning, really, if he didn't love her.

And he didn't.

Mattie thumped the pillow in a sudden excess of temper, then sagged back weakly, tears springing to her eyes. This was just going round in circles. She'd made her bed and was going to have to lie in it. The trouble was, she didn't know how on earth she was going to manage it.

CHAPTER FIVE

MATTIE slept in until just gone ten, partly because she hadn't fallen asleep until the early hours and then only managed fitful snatches and partly because she didn't want to have to face James—not after last night which, with hindsight, was deeply embarrassing.

But, confident that he would have already left for his office in the City, she pulled her cosy old quilted robe over her bunchy cotton nightie and wandered, bleary-eyed, to the kitchen in search of several cups of strong black coffee to get her kick-started.

'So there you are, madam!' Mrs Briggs' smile was warmly approving. 'I'll bring the breakfast through right away, shall I? Mr James is in the study; perhaps you would tell him?'

Mattie's heart dropped down to the soles of her small bare feet. Why had she taken his departure for the work that would always come first with him so much for granted? And it was painfully obvious from the twinkle in the housekeeper's faded brown eyes that she thought her new mistress had been sleeping off the effects of a night of steamy passion! Now she would have to face him, the thought made her feel decidedly uncomfortable.

Mattie managed the disguise of a smile, albeit a tight one as she reluctantly turned to do as she was bid. The older woman's bewildered suspicions of the day before seemed to have been allayed so she should be feeling pleased with herself. But she wasn't.

So, OK, last night she had told James that it was important that they nip possible speculation and gossip in the bud, that to the world at large they should appear as a deliriously happy newly-wedded couple.

This morning, though, she felt ashamed of herself. If they went down that road they would be living a lie, and she didn't like the idea of that. No, more than that, she hated it.

Her slender body shuddered beneath the smothering folds of her positively frumpish nightwear. She was going to have to be completely honest with him.

Well, not completely honest. She couldn't tell him how she really felt about him—it would humiliate her and embarrass him. But she could tell him he had been absolutely right. The way they conducted their marriage was no one's business but their own. They didn't have to pretend because it didn't matter what other people thought.

A complete contradiction to what she'd said last night. But then, she hadn't been herself, had she? She'd been a painted, perfumed, silly doll, pulled out of character by what Dawn had said and her own mysterious descent into stupidity.

This morning she was back to being herself. An ordinary—a very ordinary—woman, with enough brain power to recognise how stupid she'd been, and enough character to stiffen her backbone and get on with a way of life she'd allowed herself to be talked into accepting.

She could cope with being the paper wife of a man she had always adored, the only man she had ever wanted to make love with. Of course she could. She could do it because she had no other option.

But she wasn't so sure when she pushed open the study door and saw him. He looked as fiercely, compellingly male as ever. He was wearing a beautifully cut hand-crafted dark suit, his austere features dangerously uncompromising, and his potent presence sent a shaft of shuddering sensation down the entire length of her body, making her bare toes curl into the deep pile of the carpet.

He ended the call he'd been making and stood up, the height and power of him overwhelming. 'Good morning, Matts.' His smile was perfunctory, as if her late rising irritated him. 'I need to spend time at head office again today,' he told her, 'but I managed to get two tickets for The Haymarket tonight. We can go for supper.' The tone of his voice was urbane, detached, chillingly smooth. 'Breakfast?'

'Yes, Mrs Briggs said she was bringing it through,' Mattie mumbled, wishing she weren't so aware of her unalluring attire, weren't so tinglingly aware of him! 'You really needn't have waited; I overslept.' She was scurrying ahead of him, stumbling over the hem of her bulky robe, her voice breathless because he was following closely, putting her in a tail-spin.

Flinging open the breakfast-room door, she gritted her teeth. Somehow she was going to have to get back to normal, cope with the effect he always had on her. She'd done it before, very successfully; she could do it again.

'You could have eaten hours ago,' she said thinly.

'And missed the opportunity of breakfasting with

my brand-new wife? I don't think so. What would Mrs Briggs think?'

His voice was the rough-edged purr of a great jungle cat. Mattie shuddered. He had taken her misguided comments of last night on board and was acting on them. Hence this encounter and the theatre tickets. And how on earth he'd managed to get two seats for a production that was sold out for months to come was beyond her. Clout, she supposed glumly, and wondered what she thought she was doing, married but not wedded—in the strict sense of the word—to one of the world's shakers and movers.

'Here we are, then!' the housekeeper cried, trundling her heated trolley into the quiet, wood-panelled room.

Mattie swallowed a gulp of shame. The wretched contraption Mrs Briggs was pushing reminded her far too clearly of the silly charade she'd played out over dinner last night.

'Bacon, tomatoes, mushrooms, juice, toast and coffee,' Mrs Briggs recited happily, placing the offerings on the small oval table with the air of a conjurer pulling rabbits out of a hat. She beamed at them. 'Will you both be in for lunch?'

James shook his head. 'Working, I'm afraid,' he said, managing to sound suitably regretful. 'Darling?'

Mattie stared at the plate of food he'd put in front of her with shuddering distaste and felt her face flame. Calling her darling was taking things too far. He didn't mean it, and it was unnecessary. She was going to have to tell him she'd changed her mind about the garbage she'd spouted last night.

'I'll be out, too, Mrs Briggs,' she said in a squeaky voice she didn't recognise as her own. 'Shopping.'

For something suitable to wear. She should be hung, drawn and quartered for letting Dawn bully her into cramming all her old things into bags for the bin men to take away!

'And we won't be in this evening. I'm taking my wife to the theatre and we'll grab something to eat later,' James stated, pouring coffee for them both. 'So I suggest you put your feet up, take things easy.' His smile was pure charm. 'You can run along now, we're happy to look after ourselves.'

Mattie bit her lip as she caught the older woman's look of flustered pleasure. Did he know how easily he could charm the female of the species—no matter what her age or situation? Did he use it like a weapon to get what he wanted?

Whatever, this morning he was well and truly back to normal. Smooth, urbane, but definitely detached. Very different from the obviously uncomfortable male who'd confronted her last night and as good as told her to get back into the sort of things she used to wear before he jumped on her!

Before she could work out whether the frisson of wicked delight at the idea that she could, if she kept flaunting herself at him, drive him to the point of doing just that was totally out of order and thoroughly despicable, he said levelly, 'Matts, about what I said last night.'

'Hmm?' She dragged her unfocussed eyes from the view of the part of the winter-bare garden that could be seen from the tall sash window and unwillingly looked at him.

His dark brows were pulled down, his slightly hooded eyes steady. 'I was wrong to tell you what you should or should not wear. I had no right.'

It was the last thing she'd expected to hear. Colour flooded her face. 'It doesn't matter,' she cut in quickly. She didn't want to think about why he'd told her to revert to her sackcloth-and-ashes style of dress, and she didn't want him to think about it, either. For either of them to think of sex in the context of their present relationship was far too intimate. It would make her resolve to cope with the situation even more difficult than it already was.

'It does matter.' He reached for toast and spread it with butter. 'To my certain knowledge you've never given a thought to the way you look, simply pulled on the first lumpy old thing you found in the morning, tied your hair into a bunch and got on with your day.' He smiled at her across the table, as if to rob his words of any insulting intent, and Mattie grabbed her coffee-cup, cradling it with both hands.

That smile transformed his almost frighteningly strong features, revealing the compassion and the caring that very few people suspected him capable of, the side of him that had transformed the fantasy of her young love into something rock-solid and enduring.

She gulped miserably. Everything would be so much easier if he treated her like a stranger who happened to be living under his roof. Perhaps she should open her mouth and tell him as much.

But he said, leaning back in his chair now, watching her, 'I can't tell you what you should or should not wear, Matts, you have a perfect right to show yourself off as the gorgeous, striking, sexy woman that you are.'

Again that smile, accompanied by a minimal shrug of wide shoulders. 'Forget what I said last night.

Forget what you perceive my reputation to be. I don't
have uncontrollable urges to leap on every beautiful
woman I see! You're quite safe from unwanted attentions,' he added a touch dryly.

'Oh!' For the moment she could think of no other
response, her brain was whirling too fast to make the
stringing together of words that made logical sense
an impossibility.

Gorgeous, sexy, striking—his words beat at her
mind. Did he really, truly think that? But safe. From
unwanted attentions. He could take her or leave her,
was that what he was implying? But if she told him
his attentions were *wanted*, would he——?

'Oh!' she said again. Swallowed her coffee, gath-
ered herself, dragged in a breath deep enough to
swell her lungs to bursting point and decided to come
clean, to put things straight. 'Look, designer gear
isn't really my style. Quite honestly, I don't much
care what I wear. When Dawn suggested I had a
make-over, I objected at first. But then I decided to
go for it. I wondered if it was possible to—' she shot
him an agonised glance, revealing past pain '—to
look presentable; not pretty, I knew I could never be
that. But more—female. That was something I'd
given up on, you see.'

'Since when?' The silver eyes were kind now, the
long years of brotherly friendship there. Not veiled
with amusement, either, the shimmer of laughter that
had been there when viewing her ham-fisted attempts
to master anything vaguely practical.

She took heart. He was her friend, above all else
he was that. She had always been able to talk to him.
She could confide in him now.

'Since I was a scrawny, plain little thing with gingery hair and what I was told was a permanent scowl,' she answered. 'My mother despaired, poor thing. She wanted a cute, cuddly daughter and she got me instead. Then Liam was born. He was a beautiful baby, blond, blue-eyed, cute dimples, a heart-wrenching smile. I can imagine her sigh of relief when she gave up on me and turned all her attention to him.

'When she went away I knew it was partly my fault. If I'd been beautiful, like the child she'd lost, she could have loved me, and stayed with us. You see, after Liam died she couldn't bear me near her—' she was speaking earnestly, making him understand '—then when Dawn pushed me into changing my image I thought that maybe I could prove my mother wrong, prove to myself that I wasn't the ugly no-hoper she'd made me believe in.'

'You were never ugly, or a no-hoper,' James told her, the savagery in his voice carefully contained. 'You are lovely. And that is precisely why—'

'You think I should carry on wearing—'

'Exactly.' His heart kicked with an unexpectedly strong emotion. Had Mattie's mother still been alive he would have told her exactly what he thought of her. She had effectively killed her daughter's confidence in herself as a woman. The cruelty some parents inflicted on their children was beyond belief—yet not unusual, as he knew only too well.

He stood up from the table, walked round it to stand beside her. 'I have to go now. Be ready to leave at seven.' He leaned over and brushed her cheek with a kiss, and his voice was gentler than she had ever heard it. 'Finish your breakfast, Matts.'

And ten minutes later she was still there, the tips

of her fingers on the skin his lips had touched. He had never kissed her before. It hadn't been a real kiss, of course, but he hadn't been playing to the gallery, either. Affection. It was a start, wasn't it?

She hadn't got round to telling him that she'd been wrong last night, that they didn't have to pretend their marriage was something it wasn't for the benefit of other people. Tonight. She'd tell him tonight.

In the meantime, she had things to do. She didn't want him to find her too sexy, or too obvious. Affection, she thought with an upsurge of hope, was a much more solid base to build on.

Mattie put on her make-up, painstakingly recalling the instructions she'd been given. She supposed that one day it would become second nature—always provided she lived that long!

Her hand hovered over an army of lipsticks in shiny, gold-coloured tubes. She opted for the palest. Putting her steel-framed glasses on, she read the tiny label. 'Hint Of Pink.' A hint was all that was required. Forget the lush scarlets, the shimmering bronze tones, the glowing cerise that, even to her own eyes, made her mouth look like a crushed peony.

Pale pink it was, then. She applied it carefully then stood up, wincing as she pushed her aching feet into the heavy, flat black shoes that had been her final purchase of the long, dark winter afternoon.

Shopping in Oxford Street had been a nightmare. Cities always stressed her. The crowds, the traffic, the endless streets of buildings gave her claustrophobia, made her long for the open spaces, the wide skies and sheer peace of the Sussex downs.

But she was on a mission and wouldn't allow herself to give up until it was accomplished. At least Dawn wasn't with her to push her at over-the-top, far too expensive designer labels. She would stick with the chain stores.

At least she now had clothes that weren't too showy or provocative. Despite her husband's change of heart she would dress as she felt fit. Driving him to think lustful thoughts—even if he'd said he wouldn't act on them—wasn't on her agenda. If their relationship were to develop it would need more than basic animal instincts as a foundation.

If.

Suddenly swamped by negative thoughts, she eyed her reflection. Who the hell did she think she was kidding? Of course he wouldn't fall in love with her.

So, OK, he'd as good as admitted he found her sexy when she was all dressed to reveal. So what, he could handle it, hadn't he said so, only this morning? For as far back as she cared to remember he'd been swarmed over by females far more glamorous and seductive than she could ever hope to be. And he hadn't fallen in love with any of them.

Except Fiona, of course. Despite what he'd implied—that he'd picked her merely because he'd needed a wife and Fiona had fitted the bill because she was beautiful, came out of the top drawer and would be a credit to him—she didn't buy it. He had loved Fiona, he must have done, and she had hurt him badly.

So why the heck should he forget everything Fiona had meant to him and fall in love with her?

It was out of the question and she should do herself a favour and stop even thinking of the possibility.

At least he wouldn't find her even remotely sexy in this thing. A grey suit. It fitted but it didn't flatter. Everything she'd bought today had been grey, with the exception of a couple of unexciting tops in beige. Nothing startling. Startling was out.

A comb through her gleaming hair and she was ready. She kept her reading glasses on because they made her look even more staid and sensible.

She'd do.

Spot on time, she clumped downstairs to keep her theatre date with her husband.

'Do you really need to wear your glasses?' James enquired mildly as he shot out a hand to save her from blundering into a large woman wearing a fake fur stole over a shiny emerald dress.

'Of course. I do intend to read the programme.' She repressed a shiver. The warm strength of his hand made her breathing rapid and shallow.

'The stage will be a blur,' he warned. 'You won't see a thing.' Amusement enriched his voice and his fingers closed more tightly around her arm.

'You can let me go,' she snipped because she had to. Any more physical contact and she'd be wriggling into the side of his lean, hard body, melting closer and closer. She just knew she would. She wasn't made of stone. 'I'm not about to fall over my feet.'

'Looking at those shoes, I'm not so sure.'

She ignored the amused dig at her choice of footwear and wrenched her arm away. She knew he'd been silently laughing at her ever since she'd stumped into the drawing room and found him engrossed in his light reading—the financial pages of the evening newspaper. She'd seen it glittering in his eyes, heard it in his voice. Well, laughing was better than lusting. Wasn't it?

'I think we'd better find our seats,' she reminded him, peering round the thronged theatre foyer. It was years since she'd been to see a play, and that had only been in the village hall, the local school children doing *The Importance of Being Earnest*. Badly.

In an odd way she was looking forward to it. To broaden her social horizons? Or because she'd be sitting close to James, close enough to touch, close enough to revel in the spicy male scent of him, to feel his warmth?

Not a real question because she knew the answer. She despaired of herself!

She had refused to remove her reading glasses, but had perched them on the end of her nose so she could watch the stage over the top of them. Uninterested in the performance, James watched her profile, the curling sweep of her thick, long lashes, made smudgy by the dim lighting, the clear line of her neat little nose, the pout of soft lips and firm line of her jaw where the sleek fall of her hair caressed it, the poetic length of her throat.

Her obvious attempt to hide the delectable attractions of the ultra feminine body she'd only just discovered she possessed beneath the matronly grey suit, clumping shoes and steel-rimmed glasses had amused him. Now it made his heart lurch with a fierce, elemental tenderness that he had never experienced before.

Matts had certainly taken his warning about jumping on her to heart, despite the reassurances he'd given her this morning. Was she really afraid of him? Didn't she know he would never do anything to hurt her?

Silently, vehemently, he cursed his lack of control the night before. A lack of control that shamed him in more ways than one. He, who justifiably prided himself on his ability to control every aspect of his life, had lost it. The way she had looked had turned him horny. Had made him issue those crazed stipulations.

He didn't know what the hell had come over him—dammit all, it was a scant six weeks since his broken engagement had supposedly turned him off women and the messy complications of sex for the rest of his life!

Lying awake far into the night, he'd thought about it. Come to the inevitable and perfectly correct conclusion that it would be wrong—a positive crime— to force her, through the fear of the consequences, to fail to live up to her potential as a beautiful, desirable woman.

That she'd failed to listen to his countermanded instructions was evident. He would have to try harder in the reassurance department. Convince her that she had nothing to fear from him.

But—the thought hit him like an angry sledgehammer. If she could be persuaded to discard the frump additions to her wardrobe and go back to the provocative, then it was inevitable that some man would come along, fall head over heels in lust with her and take her away from him.

And she'd go—as sure as hens had feathers she'd go. Realising her full female potential went deeper than artfully applied make-up, flirty dresses, new hairstyles. It would make her want what she'd never seemed remotely interested in before—a man in her bed.

Rage possessed him, it seemed to be burning a hole in his chest, and moments before the final curtain he hussled her out of the theatre and stood on the pavement dragging the cold night air into his lungs. He needed to get her to himself, talk to her, decide whether the idea that was gripping his brain in a vice was viable or not.

Crassly, he'd believed he could handle his sexual attraction to her; he'd even rescinded his order that she stopped dressing provocatively. But, dammit, he couldn't handle it.

So he could seduce her himself, make sure no other man took his wife from him.

It would be no hardship where he was concerned. Despite his weary distaste for all women, Mattie wasn't 'all women'. Mattie was different.

But would it be a betrayal of her? The essential her?

He took her elbow, his fingers biting into the soft flesh beneath the thick grey cloth, the muscles of his hand tense. 'The restaurant's a five-minute walk away. So let's get our circulation moving.'

'James—' Sinkingly, she raked her eyes over his stony profile. Something had made him hopping mad. Boredom with the play? Or teeth-grinding aggravation because he felt he'd been forced into being seen in public with her, wasting a whole evening?

'We could go home,' she said. 'There's no need to eat out, really there isn't. You were right, we don't have to pretend. What happens, or doesn't happen, in our marriage is our business,' she assured him breathlessly, forced to trot to keep up with his rangy stride, her clumpy shoes slapping the pavement.

'We're here now.' He made a conscious effort to relax and felt something melt inside him as he smiled down into her troubled face. He didn't want her to be troubled; he wanted the poor scrap to be happy.

But she wasn't a poor scrap, was she?

The brisk exercise had painted her cheeks with wild-rose colour, the cold air making her eyes sparkle like golden jewels. And that dull grey suit and the fawn woolly thing she was wearing beneath it didn't make her any less gorgeous. His eyes had been opened as far as Mattie was concerned and he wanted her.

But would wanting be enough for her?

Somehow, this evening, he was going to try to find out. Try to lay the foundation for a future together that was far different from the one they had embarked on.

His hand slid down to take hers. 'Let's eat,' he said thickly. 'I'm ravenous.' Ravenous for her. But would she, could she, feel the same?

If she did it would be the icing on the no-nonsense cake of their marriage. Nothing was more certain than that.

He felt her slim fingers curl around his and something fiercely protective twisted inside him. Whatever happened he wouldn't rush her into something she didn't feel was right for her.

They were shown to the table he'd automatically insisted on reserving, a softly lit alcove partially screened from the main body of the classy restaurant by the fronds of sweetly scented jasmine, intertwined with the arching, feathery leaves of a miniature date palm.

A perfect setting for a romantic dinner for two, Mattie thought miserably. Right down to the white camellias floating in a crystal bowl, the flickering candle, the champagne on ice. He must have ordered it when he'd reserved a table. If she drank any she'd get silly. She couldn't afford to get silly.

Somehow she had to convince him that there was no need for all this. What she'd said to him last night was nonsense; she hadn't thought it through. Pretending they were a loving couple, sharing a candlelit meal was agony because she so desperately wanted it to be true.

The champagne cork was drawn. Mattie flinched. Glanced at the menu and ordered the first thing her eyes lighted on, and gave him a firm look from behind her lenses when he handed her a flute of the foaming wine and ordered softly, 'Relax, Mattie.'

'I'll try,' she promised, not at all sure she could fulfil.

They were alone now, both waiters gone, alone with soft lights, the seductive scent of jasmine. Alone with her growing need to reach out and touch him...

She cleared her throat briskly, settled her glasses more firmly on the bridge of her nose, and said with genuine commiseration. 'You don't have to put yourself through this kind of charade. I'm sure you must hate it. You were right, I was wrong. We don't need to pretend.'

'No pretence. I'm enjoying this.' The beautifully proportioned fingers of one hand were curled around the slender stem of his wineglass, the immaculately cut jacket of his dark suit emphasising the breadth

of his shoulders, the grey eyes smoky, the carved line
of his mouth made smoulderingly sensual, courtesy
of the subdued lighting, she supposed. And he was
only saying that for her sake. What had she said the
night before?

Absently, she took a gulp of champagne, and remembered. She'd told him she didn't want to be
sneered at because she was married to a man who
didn't fancy her at all.

That was why he was pretending to enjoy himself
now. For her sake! Her heart lurched and twisted.
The effort he was making only made her love him
more. How deeply could you love a man who didn't
love you back and still retain your sanity?

'And I want you to enjoy it, too.' He leaned forward slightly. 'Enjoy the experience of being out on
the town with your husband.'

But he wasn't, not truly her husband. But she
wanted him to be. Her throat went dry. Why was he
looking at her as if she were the only woman in the
world for him when nothing could be further from
the truth?

She said, her voice sounding strangled, 'It's not
really my scene. I feel out of place.'

'Shh—' He laid a finger over the soft, rose-petal
pink of her mouth to silence her, dragged in a
charged breath as he felt the silky smoothness, the
quivering softness of her lips beneath his touch, and
told himself harshly to cool it. There was no rush.
None at all. That was what his brain said. His body
had other ideas.

His body had to learn to wait.

'You can fit into any scene you want to be in.' He
replaced his hand on the stem of his wineglass, hold-

ing her lovely eyes with his. 'And there's no need for either of us to lay down hard and fast rules. Let's look on our relationship as a voyage of discovery, relax, see where it takes us.'

It was as far as he could go towards sowing the seed of future intimacy in her mind. As far as he dared go at the moment. With Mattie he would have to tread carefully; she hadn't the worldly-wise sophistication to be anything other than scared witless if he told her he had changed his mind, that he wanted sex in their marriage on top of everything else.

He saw the quickening of the pulse that beat at the base of her throat, saw the question that leapt in the translucent gold of her eyes, wondered how best to answer if she gave it voice and inwardly cursed as their first course arrived, breaking the moment.

And could have beat both fists on the table, scattering dishes to kingdom come when a drift of heavy perfume, the spike of a cut-glass accent invaded their space.

'Darling—I caught a glimpse of you at the theatre and guessed you'd come on here. It's what we always did, after Haymarket, one of our special places—you bad thing!' A tinkling laugh that carried no warmth. 'I heard the unbelievable rumour. I simply had to find out if it was true—that you actually went and married— Oh, hi, Matilda, so we meet again. What a scream! Goodness, you've cut off some of that hair!'

Mattie felt ill. She was sure her face had turned green. She wanted to hide, fall through the floor. Dressing down, very down, had backfired on her.

James would be comparing the two of them and feeling as ill as she was!

She had only met Fiona Campbell-Blair that one time, when James had brought her to Berrington to introduce her as his fiancée. She'd been the house guest from hell and both Mattie and her father had ended up disliking her intensely.

But looking at her—tall, elegant, so very beautiful, the pale satin sheath she was wearing showing her voluptuous figure to stunning advantage—she could see why James had wanted her as his wife.

But she'd jilted him and he'd married on the rebound, got himself landed with a very poor second best.

Courteously, he'd risen to his feet. Fiona was standing close to him. Too close? Yes, Mattie decided. Much too close. And he was hurting. James never showed his feelings but now his face was tight with some painful emotion, his lithe body tense.

Bristling, Mattie wanted to slap the other woman. Hard. Why couldn't the hateful creature leave him in peace to get over her as best he could? Why eat up his features with those hard blue eyes, pout her lips at him as if she were waiting for his kiss? Why rub salt in his still-raw wounds?

'Are you intending to join us? Or do you enjoy standing around so that other people can't eat?' Mattie asked with a withering rudeness that was completely alien to her.

'What?' Fiona gave her a look that conveyed the surprise of a woman who'd just been spoken to by an inanimate piece of furniture. 'Good Lord, no! I'm with my own party.' She tipped her blonde head on one side, a half-smile playing round her mouth as she trailed the fingertips of one hand down the stony cheek of the man she'd so cruelly and publicly rejected. 'Just had to totter over to give my congratulations. I take it they are in order, James?' Her tone implied the precise opposite. '*Ciao*, darling. Be happy. If you can!'

CHAPTER SIX

THE rest of the evening was a wash-out. The food was barely touched and the champagne went flat. Mattie was making uncomfortable small talk and James did his best to respond but knew he was failing miserably.

'I'll get someone to find us a taxi,' he said when the silences between the spurts of stilted conversation became distinctly edgy.

Abruptly, he beckoned their waiter over, asking for the bill. The evening was unsalvageable while his mind was frantically trying to make some sense out of what was happening here.

He'd learned at an early age that emotions made you vulnerable; they were counter-productive, a waste of time and energy, energy that could be used along much more useful and controllable lines. It was a lesson he'd learned well.

So why, since Fiona's interruption, was he in the remorseless grip of what had to be the mother and father of all emotion? It was anger, he recognised. Because Fiona had spoiled the mood of the evening? Because the wretched woman had sunk her barbs into Mattie, hurting her? Couple that with a fierce, gut-wrenching need to protect Mattie from anything and anyone who could hurt her and he was landed with something he was going to have to get his head around.

Wryly he noted the wash of relief that flooded her

expressive features at his ending of the evening that had become so awkward for both of them. He slid his plastic credit card back into his wallet and told her flatly, 'I'll be flying out to Jerez tomorrow. The new hotel and leisure complex, remember?'

The ground work had been done, the deal signed and sealed. His site manager and the firm's architect could manage perfectly adequately without him; nevertheless, he'd be with them in the company's Lear jet tomorrow.

It would give him the necessary time and space to get his head straight, decide whether he and Mattie had a future together. Fiona's brief intrusion, the unprecedented emotions it had aroused, had turned everything upside down.

'For long?' Mattie asked, trying not to sound too relieved about it.

She really did need some time without his forceful presence, time alone to get this feeling of draining misery under control. Before Fiona's arrival she'd had the distinct feeling that he'd been suggesting that, some day in the future, their marriage could have become a real one, that he could have learned to love her.

A voyage of discovery, he'd said. It could have led anywhere.

But she'd been so wrong. He'd only had to see his ex-fiancée again, a reminder of what he'd lost—and a hammering home of what he'd actually got—for his relaxed, warm mood to change to something terse, unfalteringly abstracted. He couldn't even pretend to be enjoying her company.

'Difficult to say.' He stood up, moving round to pull out her chair for her, wondering bitterly how he could ever have entertained the thought that he could seduce her, take her to his bed and after that everything would be hunky-dory, uncomplicated.

Life wasn't like that, unfortunately. She deserved more than that. And he needed time to look deep inside himself and discover if the emotions he'd always steered well clear of, and had so recently hit him for six, were lasting and true. For both their sakes he had to find the answer to that.

He watched as Mattie scrabbled about beneath the table for her handbag, whipping the unnecessary disguise of her reading glasses off her nose, dropping them into the bag's capacious depths. 'I'll keep you posted, of course,' he told her. 'And if you really don't want to get back to your work just yet you could fill your time by helping with your father's move.'

That could be weeks away! Mattie's eyes widened with something approaching panic. Was he planning on staying away that long? Why? Because after seeing Fiona again he couldn't bear to be anywhere near the woman he'd married on the rebound? Was he only now realising what a terrible mistake he'd made?

If he hadn't leapt into this ill-considered paper marriage he could have bent his considerable will into the challenge of getting Fiona back. Was that what he was brooding on?

He'd already left before she surfaced the next morning. The house felt empty without him. She thought about contacting the agency, asking if they had anything for her, but knew she wouldn't be able to concentrate her mind on anything cerebral. She acted on James' parting advice instead and phoned her father.

Everything was moving more quickly than they'd dared to hope. The Sussex house had been on the market for less than forty-eight hours before they'd had a firm offer for the full asking price and the apartment near Sloane Square was secured. The formalities had been dealt with very quickly and it wouldn't be long before they moved to London. So, yes, her help would be much appreciated.

Helping her father and Mrs Flax—'Call me Emily'—decide what should go to the apartment, what go to auction, and what should be thrown out, helped take her mind off James' prolonged absence and the probable reason for it.

But her father said, making her flinch, 'If James knew he would be spending this amount of time in Spain—and I honestly don't see why he should because there's no problem as far as I know—then he should have taken you with him. It would have gone some way to making up for not giving you a honeymoon.'

'I didn't want to go,' Mattie answered quickly. It wasn't a lie. If he'd offered—and they didn't need to know he hadn't—she would have declined. She needed time to accept the fact that she would never take Fiona's place in his heart and decide whether she had the necessary strength of mind to go on with this charade of a marriage.

They were sitting in the kitchen, surrounded by packing cases because they'd be moving out tomorrow. And Emily Flax, taking a casserole out of the oven, said comfortably, 'I agree with you. Home's the best place to be at this time of the year unless you're heading for the opposite side of the globe and the sun.' She put the heavy dish on the centre of the table and suggested firmly, 'Edward, I think it's time, don't you?'

'What? Oh, yes, yes—of course.' He looked flustered, fiddled with his cutlery. His voice was hoarse. He cleared his throat. 'Mattie, Emily and I have something to tell you—' He dropped his fork.

'You're getting married. Congratulations!' she smiled, happy for them, staunchly refusing to be miserable for herself. 'When?'

'How did you know?' He retrieved his fork from the floor and straightened, his face red, and Emily said lightly, 'Women have a nose for these things, isn't that right, Mattie? And we decided on an April wedding. Paris in spring for a honeymoon. It's not too far to travel, and there's so much we both want to see. Could you open the wine, Edward, while I dish up?' The look they exchanged was nothing short of doting, the sudden shrilling of the wall-mounted phone an unwelcome intrusion.

'I'll get it,' Mattie said. 'It's probably the removal people confirming their time of arrival in the morning.'

But it wasn't. It was James. He'd phoned punctiliously, once a week, and as his last call had been two days ago she hadn't been expecting to hear from him. And she returned to the table a few minutes later, her heart thumping.

'It was James,' she said. Then took a deep breath to steady herself. 'He'll be home in six days' time, and the day after that we're flying out to Barbados and staying there for a month. He's rented a house on one of the small islands, apparently.'

He hadn't said why, or told her what was in his mind. Just asked her if her passport was in order, told her to shop for suitable clothes. He'd sounded so matter of fact.

Mattie resumed her place at the table and let the enthusiastic comments over the belated but romantic honeymoon destination go over her head.

Why, after keeping well away from her for weeks, had he decided he could spare a whole month out of his busy working life to be with her?

Unless he wanted her well away from everyone who knew them before he told her that he now realised their paper marriage had been a mistake, that he wanted to end it. It was the only thing she could think of that made any kind of sense. It most certainly wasn't because they were a normal, recently married couple and he wanted weeks of her undiluted company!

The breakdown of their marriage, coming so soon after the public and humiliating rejection Fiona had subjected him to, and the resultant publicity, would be something he would find utterly distasteful.

Perhaps he wanted her help in the damage limitation department.

The thought was deeply depressing.

'Feeling better?'

Behind closed eyelids Mattie's mind was drifting in neutral, fuzzy round the edges. But the soft concern of his voice, the touch of cool fingers on her forehead as he moved a tangle of rumpled hair to one side, made her come fully awake, shamefully aware of the nuisance she'd made of herself.

She opened her eyes slowly. The big double bed

was comfy and she was covered by a white cotton cut-work spread, and the room was blessedly cool, many long windows with the bright Caribbean sunlight slanting downwards through the partially closed hardwood louvres, making the pale sage green decor misty by contrast.

'James,' she managed thickly. Bending over her, his face was shadowed, dark brows drawn down, but there was a hint of a smile on his sensual mouth. What on earth would he be thinking of her? That her behaviour was par for the course—that he couldn't have expected anything else from his gauche, unsophisticated wife?

She shuddered inside. Fiona wouldn't have been airsick, she wouldn't have come within a whisker of passing out in the transit lounge of Barbados' airport, or thrown up again on the scary helicopter flight out to this island. She wouldn't have arrived a sweaty, crumpled wreck, barely able to stand.

Fiona would have taken it all in her stride, lapped up the first-class nine-hour flight, sipping champagne, making witty, clever conversation. But then Fiona wouldn't have been feeling ill with apprehension, wondering if her marriage was about to end.

Mattie groaned. 'Is it tomorrow yet?' she asked stupidly.

The smile in his voice told her he'd registered the silliness of her question, but he didn't answer it, simply asked again, 'How do you feel? You've slept for hours.'

How did she feel? Mattie sat up against the white-covered pillows to find out and only when she saw the sinfully seductive yet intent gaze of his eyes did she glance down and discover she was naked, the twin pertly rounded globes of her breasts the focus of his complete attention.

Flustered, she jerked at the spread to cover herself. The caress of his eyes had been like a physical touch, almost as if his hands had shaped and discovered her, his mouth suckled the rosy tips. Already her breasts had hardened, her whole body on fire, pulsing with need.

She smothered another groan. Somehow she was going to have to cope with the way she ached for him, wanted him, needed him. Their marriage was going nowhere; it was about to end—she was certain of that now. She could think of no other reason for his sudden desire to take them both out of circulation for an entire month.

'Did you put me to bed?' She injected asperity into her tone but inside she felt as if she were coming unstitched, imagining his hands on her body, his eyes. She couldn't remember much about their arrival apart from a headache that had felt as if her scalp had been split in half, the tablets he had given her, him carrying her up the stairs.

'No, Mercy did. Under the circumstances, I thought it best.'

The brusqueness of his tone made her shiver, the way he stepped back from the bedside, thrusting his hands into the pockets of the light cotton jeans he was wearing, his wide shoulders rigid beneath the black sleeveless vest, distancing him.

Under the circumstances of their crazy marriage he wouldn't want any physical contact. It made sense. 'And who is Mercy?' she asked lightly, refusing to let him know how much the death of even the smallest, stubbornly lingering hope could hurt.

'Mercy and her husband Manuel look after everything here. They come with the territory—which is ours for the next month.' He strode round the room with the loose-limbed grace that was so characteristic of him, opening the louvres, letting the light flood in. 'She will be bringing your breakfast shortly.' He turned back to her, a flash of silver in his narrowed eyes. 'After you've eaten—not before—' he stressed, 'you can shower and dress. Wear something light, the temperature's soaring. We'll spend the day quietly, give you time to fully recover.'

Recover, she thought blisteringly as he walked out of the room. Be fit and strong enough to take what he had to tell her, that he wanted to end their marriage as seamlessly as possible, discuss tactics—perhaps he would spend most of his time away, on far-flung construction sites, while she sat quietly at home, so that their eventual divorce wouldn't raise a single eyebrow because their separateness would have been accepted.

He wouldn't tell her the real reason—that after seeing Fiona again he couldn't bear to have another woman take her place, even nominally. That he wanted to be free to pursue the woman he did love, persuade her to change her mind about marrying him. He was far too urbane for that. His emotions too carefully guarded.

Well, she had news for him! She couldn't go on this way, either, swinging between hope and despair; wanting him, always wanting him, was driving her mad.

And she was already recovered and he couldn't tell her what to do. She slid her legs out of bed to prove it, swayed alarmingly, gritted her teeth and tottered to the *en suite* bathroom, admiring the pale green marble, the spotlessly gleaming chrome, the sparkling glass door of the shower cubicle, the shelves and shelves of lotions and essences.

Showering and brushing her teeth made her feel much better. A tray had been left on a table beneath one of the windows, so Mercy must have been here while she was in the bathroom.

The rich aroma of hot coffee teased her nostrils but she ignored it for now and dressed in a simple light blue gauzy cotton skirt and a plain white T-shirt first, then drank her coffee, too wound up to sit, staring out of the window over an expanse of closely mown emerald-green grass to the sea that lapped against a white, crescent-shaped cove.

She closed the louvres. She wasn't about to be seduced by paradise. She was going to be tough. Tough enough to go along with whatever he had to say to her.

The eggs Benedict beneath the domed cover she lifted turned her stomach but she forced down some of the fruit as a token gesture, then hunted for her flat canvas shoes. Mercy must have unpacked last night. All her things were neatly hung, her underwear and nightwear folded in drawers.

As were his. Mercy wouldn't have known, of course, that they occupied separate rooms. No doubt James would discreetly move his stuff today.

James. Despite having talked herself into a state of common sense, she felt her stomach tighten at the thought of facing him, talking things through.

But she had to do it. Now.

Straightening her spine, she walked out of the

room, down a broad curving flight of polished wood stairs and found Mercy instead.

A small, curvy woman, in her mid-forties, Mattie guessed, admiring the smooth, coffee-coloured skin, patrician features and bright dark eyes. She looked efficient, imperturbable, nice to have around. She said, her accent faintly Spanish, 'I hope you have got over the effects of your long flight—I know how disorientating such journeys can be.' Her smile was sympathetic. Mattie took to her immediately, feeling marginally more relaxed.

'I'm absolutely fine, thanks,' and then, because she had to, 'I'm looking for my husband. Have you seen him?'

'He's waiting on the terrace, by the pool. I will show you.' She led the way through an airy room, full of sunlight, with tall French windows open to the sea breeze, explaining, 'It is best you use the pool until you learn which beaches give safe bathing. Some have reefs which protect them from wild seas and sharks, some have not. Manuel will tell you.'

'I'll stay with the pool!' Mattie answered with a lightness she was far from feeling. Every step she took brought her nearer to him, every second that passed brought her nearer to the time when she would hear him tell her that everything was over.

'I will bring fresh coffee out in a moment. And fruit juice, yes?'

Mattie heard what Mercy was saying but could only nod in abstracted reply, blink the film of moisture from her eyes, force herself to focus on the sparkling waters of the huge outdoor pool, the mellow stone paving of the terrace backed by flame trees, their branches covered with vivid scarlet blossoms.

And the man who was waiting. James, indolently stretched out on a padded lounger, his hair slicked to his skull, the skin that covered his tautly muscled body spangled with droplets of water, his only concession to modesty skin-tight black swimming briefs.

How on earth could she hope to keep a clear head, a cool mind, be able to discuss their future rationally when every power-packed inch of that perfectly formed and honed male body was an open invitation to touch, a temptation too far?

But then when had life ever been fair?

It was up to her to do the best she could.

'Mattie—'

Mercy's voice must have alerted him to her presence. She hadn't moved a muscle herself. She could hardly breathe.

He sat up, swinging his long legs over the side of the lounger. The olive tone of his skin was darkened by a very male dusting of body hair. She still couldn't breathe.

'You look much better.' Approval in his voice, but there was no smile. His mouth was tight, as if he were gritting his teeth. She was sure there were lines of strain on his lean, handsome face and his eyes were unreadable behind the dark sunglasses he was wearing.

So he, too, was finding the situation difficult. She knew he was far from being a callous man—he would find it hard to tell her that the simple, mutually undemanding partnership he'd mooted when he'd proposed marriage was now unacceptable, that he wanted her out of his life as soon as was discreetly possible.

Bitter-sweet compassion twisted sharply inside

her. She longed to take his face between her hands, kiss away those betraying tension lines. But she couldn't do that. Instead she would have to make this as easy as possible for him, pretend that his change of mind didn't matter to her.

'Don't hover.' He managed to raise a smile of sorts. 'Sit here, out of the sun.' He indicated the other lounger, separated from the one he was using by a low table, completely in the shade of a huge flower-patterned parasol. 'I don't want your skin to burn.'

Not much danger of that, Mattie thought dully. Unlike him, she was modestly covered. But the blue waters of the huge pool looked cool and tempting. He had obviously been swimming and had things been different she would have shot back to her room, pulled on her swimsuit and plunged straight in.

But things weren't different and she couldn't stand here for ever, like an intruder at a stranger's party. She made her feet move, the light breeze moulding the fine fabric of her skirt to her thighs, her heart sinking to the pit of her stomach.

'I need to talk to you,' he told her as she perched gingerly on the edge of the vacant lounger, as if it were made of spun sugar and would shatter beneath her weight.

Crunch time, she thought, her mouth going dry, her heart pumping. She wanted to run away and hide. She didn't want to hear this. And almost sobbed with relief when Mercy appeared. Reprieve, if only for a few moments.

The tray that was deposited on the low table held a pot of fresh coffee, cups, cream and sugar. A tall jug of fruit juice, glasses, an insulated container of ice cubes. 'Oh, lovely, thank you, Mercy!' she babbled, aware of the hot tide of hysteria rising inside her. 'Isn't this nice, James? Will you have coffee, or juice?'

Aware that Mercy was beginning to turn away Mattie didn't wait for his answer. 'What time would you like to serve lunch, Mercy? What time would suit you best? Something light, I think, don't you? In this heat!' She wished, she wished she could shut up! She could babble for hours but it wouldn't alter the inevitable.

Delaying it wouldn't make it any easier to bear. Besides, the tension was killing her! Best to get it over with. Out in the open, then she'd know where she stood. While they were still legally married she would always hope; she wouldn't be able to help it. So ending it would be the best way for her, in the long run.

'One o'clock will be fine, Mercy.' The sound of his voice alerted her to the fact that the other woman had been saying something. Mattie hadn't heard a word. She'd been too busy chasing her own thoughts round and round in her head, the internal din they'd been making drowning out every other sound. Except his voice.

Mercy had retreated. So this was it. With a conscious effort she raised her head, scooped her hair away from her face with both hands and said flatly, 'You had something to say to me.'

'I have.' The long line of his mouth was tight. He removed his sunglasses and put them on the table, next to the tray. She could see his eyes now but they told her nothing. The silver gaze was steady, half obscured by the hooded lids and heavy black lashes.

'Well?' she prompted, desperately holding herself

together, hoping she didn't look as shatteringly apprehensive as she felt.

He was leaning forward now, tanned forearms resting along the length of his tautly muscled thighs. Mattie kept her eyes glued to his. If she let them wander to the breadth of his shoulders, the wide firm chest, the washboard-tight midriff, and down to the skimpy briefs that clung to the essence of his masculinity she would be lost, a gibbering, pleading, weeping wreck.

'There's no easy way to tell you this,' he said sombrely. His brows knotted in a frown. 'Before we married we made a bargain. I have to tell you, Mattie, I find I'm unable to stick with it.'

She felt the blood drain out of her face. She closed her eyes. She felt sick. Hadn't she guessed, known, this was about to happen? And hadn't she told herself she would make it as easy for him as she could?

She huffed in a shallow breath, unscrewed her eyelids and told him thinly, 'I understand.'

'No, I don't think you do.' His voice was lower now, gentler. 'I saw our marriage as an oasis of peace with the business safely under the umbrella of our union. Our lives running companionably along parallel lines—no meeting point in the physical sense— no sex to muddy the waters. You went along with that, and it's probably what you still want. Expect. Am I right?'

She had no idea what he was getting at and, in any case, she was incapable of answering. She simply blinked at him, her lips falling apart. Oh, she might have gone along with his idea of a marriage of convenience, kidding herself that she could be content. But how could she tell him that she wanted him in every way there was with every atom of her being?

'I know I'm right,' he answered his own questions, his voice heavy. 'When I warned you of the probable consequences if you continued to dress provocatively you couldn't jump back into your old style of dressing fast enough! But I have to be honest with you, we both deserve that much—Matts, I want you. If you went around wearing an old sack, I'd still want to take you to bed. I can't live like that—wanting to make love to you yet having to keep to the letter of our bargain. And I don't imagine it would be something you'd be comfortable with, either.

'So we make our marriage a real one, or we end it. It's up to you to decide which way you want to go. No rush.' There was a hollow look in his eyes, a downward twist to his mouth. 'We have four weeks here, time enough for you to make up your mind. I won't put any pressure on you; whatever happens it will be your decision entirely.'

For a moment he looked achingly vulnerable. Then he pulled himself to his feet. 'You look stunned,' he said dryly. 'I'm sorry. I'll leave you in peace to think it over.'

CHAPTER SEVEN

MATTIE watched him go, her heart pounding in her chest. As before, when he'd asked her to marry him, she couldn't believe her own ears. She must have misheard, or misunderstood. Her brain had suffered some sort of burn-out. She was going crazy!

How could he possibly want to make love to her when the gorgeous, ultra-sophisticated Fiona had once shared his bed? Unless, of course, that was precisely the reason.

He wanted to use her to drive the memory of the woman he still loved out of his head.

The bargain they'd made was a non-starter because he was a normal, virile male.

He needed sex.

And she'd do.

She felt her face go red and abstractedly poured fruit juice into one of the tall glasses. Then stared at it. She didn't want it, and, even if she did, there was a lump in her throat the size of Snowdon and she wouldn't be able to swallow a single drop of it.

She wanted him to make love to her, oh, of course she did. Just thinking about it made liquid flames ignite deep inside her.

But she was going to have to think this out. Rationally. Take a leaf from his book and not allow her emotions to rule her head.

She got to her feet, took a deep breath and followed him. She knew his integrity of old; all she had

to do was ask the question. Ask him if he'd be using
her in an attempt to drive the memory of Fiona out
of his head.

Because, if he was, it wouldn't work.

She knew there was no way she could be favour-
ably compared to the fabulous, sophisticated woman
he had really wanted to marry, and it followed that
if it came down to it he would find her a poor bed
mate. An inexperienced virgin. Without love on his
part it would be a disaster and could only make everything so very much worse.

If she followed her emotions and let him make
love to her he would feel himself tied. Trapped. He
was an honourable man without a cruel bone in his
body—he would hardly turn around then, tell her
their marriage wasn't working, and ask for a divorce.

She negotiated the length of the sprawling white
villa and turned onto the sweep of emerald-green
grass. He could have gone inside by the main entrance, but somehow she didn't think so.

The heat seemed oppressive now and her T-shirt
was sticking to her body. She pushed her hair out of
her eyes with the back of one hand and glanced
around. Twin stone pillars marked the transition between the driveway and the track that led, she
guessed, down to the small village and harbour she'd
seen from the helicopter yesterday. He would hardly
have gone that way, dressed as he was.

Mattie headed seawards. A short flight of wooden
steps led down to the sheltered cove. The silvery
sand curved in a crescent, an empty crescent. The
fluttering inside her subsided to a dull ache of disappointment then began in earnest again, tying her

stomach in knots as she saw him cleaving through the jade-green waters, far out.

She lifted a hand to shade her eyes from the painful glare of the sun, watching him, her teeth biting into her lower lip. Mercy had talked of sharks. Fear closed its icy fingers round her heart.

Stupid! she chided herself. He knows what he's doing, he always does. Foolish to think, even for a moment, that she was watching a man who was trying to outpace some private demons. James wasn't like that. He was merely using up some of that boundless energy of his while giving her time to think about what he'd said.

And because his emotions weren't in play, he wouldn't be too bothered about her answer.

He wasn't as 'off women' as he'd believed himself to be. Sex was important to him, after all. It had only taken a few weeks of celibacy for him to come to that conclusion.

If she wouldn't oblige then their strange marriage would be over and he'd turn to one of the lovely young creatures who hung around him.

With a dredging sigh of relief she saw him strike back towards the shore. Her shoulders relaxed and just as suddenly her mind became as crystal clear as the stretch of glittering waters that lay between them.

His reasons for wanting to make their marriage a real one no longer mattered. Forget the ethics of the situation, they weren't important.

She wasn't a cowering mouse, she was a full-blooded woman and he was her husband. And she loved him enough for both of them, enough to make up for his lack in that department.

Kicking off her canvas shoes, she walked slowly

into the water, heading towards him, and when the wavelets reached her waist she stopped, watching his powerful crawl, the dedication he was bringing to the expending of energy. And when a wave, higher than the rest, soaked her T-shirt, she gasped, feeling her breasts harden, her nipples peak against the wet fabric.

He saw her then, she knew he did, because he changed to a lazy side stroke, his eyes on her as he slowly drew closer, almost as if he didn't want her breaking his solitude.

Still yards away, he stood up, slicked back his wet hair with one hand, and all she could see was the tension in his powerful body and all she could hear was the thunder of her heartbeats, the gentle lapping of the water until, long moments later, he said, 'What are you doing?'

A fair question. Fully dressed and up to her waist in water! She felt her lips curve. 'Making a symbolic gesture—meeting you halfway.' And held out her arms.

'Matts—' He began to move towards her and she could see the stark query in his eyes. She pushed through the water, reaching him, her hands touching his shoulders, feeling the silky tightness of his warm skin, the tautly defined muscles that lay beneath with the tips of her fingers.

His breathing was as shallow and rapid as her own, his stomach muscles clenched. Mattie's toes curled into the sandy bed of the sea and her body shook with fine, helpless tremors.

'Kiss me,' she invited, her voice breathless, and saw his eyes darken.

'You want me to?' he asked softly. But he didn't

reach out to touch her; his hands were clenched into fists at his side.

Love gave Mattie the courage she needed. Her hands slipped from his shoulders, captured one of the fists and slowly unclenched his fingers, her eyes intent on what she was doing. 'Can't you tell?' She lifted his hand and placed it on one engorged breast, the peaking nipple telling the truth, and she heard the harsh drag of his breath, saw the deep shudder that swept through his body.

'You've thought this out?' The hand that had so briefly held her breast dropped back to his side. 'It wasn't an ultimatum, Mattie,' he said flatly. 'Just a statement of fact. I want a full marriage, but I don't want you to agree to something you would be unhappy about.'

'You're not making this easy,' she muttered, feeling faintly ridiculous and very awkward.

Her attempt to show him that she wanted him must have been so clumsy and gauche. She wished she had a tenth of the experience of the Fionas of this world, then it would have been so easy. 'I would like our marriage to be a full one, too,' she mumbled. 'I can't express it more plainly than that.'

Her shoulders tense, she turned, pushed her way through the limpid water towards the white sands of the curving bay. She felt like weeping. She'd imagined a very different outcome when she'd walked out towards him.

She'd offered herself to him and now he was acting as if he wanted her to change her mind, making it all sound so calculated and clinical.

A sob built in her chest, making her shoulders slump, but it changed into a gasp as he caught her from behind, twisting her round in a flurry of salt water, his hands moving upwards to position her head beneath his.

His sensually modelled mouth was a whisper away from hers. She felt her lips part, quiver, and time stood still until he closed the tiny distance and took her mouth with his own and then everything exploded with a hunger so savage it shook her to the depths of her soul.

The tidal wave of pleasure melted her into his body, had her clinging helplessly to him, drowning in a sea of exquisite sensation and when he at last broke the kiss he sounded as shaken as she felt when he told her, 'I think we'd better go back to the house, don't you?' He released her hands from their stranglehold around his neck and she tried to get her eyes to focus properly.

His kiss had been everything she'd ever dreamed it would be. And more. But he had been unwilling to prolong it while she had wanted it to go on for ever. Had she been too eager? Did sophisticated women kiss differently?

But the look he gave her when he slipped an arm around her waist as they waded through the final stretch of water sent her hurtling back into a state of delirium, her knees almost buckling beneath her when he said softly, 'I want complete privacy when I finally make love to my wife. I want a soft bed beneath us and all the time in the world to explore every inch of her body. To touch and taste and finally possess.'

She would never have made it back to the room she'd woken in this morning without his support. Her legs felt as if her bones had turned to wobbly rubber and her breath came in irregular, shallow snatches. The battle between paralysing nervousness and wild sexual excitement which was taking place inside her was pulling her to pieces, giving her a panic attack!

The bed had been freshly made, the remains of the barely touched breakfast removed and bowls of sweetly scented flowers adorned the bedside tables. But there had been far deeper changes than that since she'd walked out of this room a couple of hours ago, convinced that he was about to tell her their marriage was over.

Changes that were far-reaching, almost terrifying in their enormity.

Could she handle them? She really didn't know.

She tried to breathe deeply to calm herself but shivered instead, and James frowned slightly, turned off the air-conditioning unit and said, 'Get out of those wet things, Mattie, you look cold.' He was smiling gently but his eyes were veiled. She couldn't tell what he was really thinking. 'Or are you simply petrified? Don't worry, I'm not about to act like a caveman. We'll take everything slowly. And if you change your mind, you only have to tell me. OK? Now,' he added prosaically, 'I suggest we shower the salt off before lunch.'

He stripped off his swimming briefs and walked through to the bathroom. No false modesty, Mattie thought, her mouth dry as she watched, hypnotised by his potent male beauty, terrified by the strength of her love for him and the almost certain knowledge that when he did get around to making love with her she would be a huge disappointment to him.

She could hear the sound of the shower and she longed to have the confidence, the *savoir-faire* to strip off and join him. She gritted her teeth, willing herself to move, but she couldn't and she was still there, her eyes wild with something like panic now, when he walked back in, towelling his hair.

He was perfection. Her throat closed up; she could barely breathe. Her face felt frozen.

He gave her a long, assessing look and tossed the damp towel aside. 'This isn't going to work, is it, Matts?' He sounded weary. 'When we kissed on the shore I thought it would, that you meant what you'd said. But right now, approaching crunch time, you look as if you're about to be fastened into the electric chair. I should have remembered how you always fell in with other people's wishes. Dawn's make-over plans—' bitterness spiked his voice as he went on '—my marriage proposal, and the restrictions I initially placed on it. My suggestion this morning that we consummate it.'

He was pulling drawers out now, eventually finding what he was looking for and flinging a pair of stone-coloured cotton shorts onto the bed. 'As I said, I don't expect you to do anything you'd be unhappy with. So we forget the whole thing. OK? I'll move my gear into another room. I might want you but I'm not about to turn you into a martyr.'

This was dreadful! A tear streaked down Mattie's pale face and the scalding heat of it reminded her that she was a living breathing creature, that she could move, she could speak. And she could be as honest with him as he'd been with her.

She couldn't tell him the whole truth—that she was in love with him, had been for years. He wouldn't want her to dump that on him. But she could explain everything else.

She said, her voice sounding quavery, 'I'm not terrified of you. Or of making love with you.' A faint flush crept over her skin and there was a prickling sensation in the most intimate parts of her body. Just talking about making love with him turned her on.

He had his back to her, the long muscles clenching as he fastened the waistband of his shorts around his narrow waist. She saw his wide shoulders lift in an uninterested shrug, as if he didn't believe what she'd said.

'To tell you the truth, I'm simply afraid of being one huge disappointment,' she told him more firmly. 'I'm completely inexperienced, and compared to—' she couldn't bear to say that name, to remind him unnecessarily of the woman who must be almost constantly in his thoughts, so she substituted 'the sort of girlfriends you've had in the past, I'm no oil painting.'

There, she'd said it. Put her fears out in the open. And her words had grabbed his whole attention. He went very still then slowly turned to face her. Undoing the fastening of his hip-hugging shorts he let them fall to the floor.

'Mattie,' he ground out, his eyes dark, 'if your mother were still alive she'd have a hell of a lot to answer for. You have got to learn to stop putting yourself down. Come here.'

It was a command, but softly spoken. Mattie went. His silver eyes held hers intently for several breathtaking moments before his hands slid to the button at the waistband of her skirt. Dealing with it, he slid the wet and clammy garment down until it pooled around her feet, then peeled off her damp T-shirt.

Did he realize just how erotic this was? Mattie

asked herself wildly as he knelt in front of her, hooking his thumbs beneath her briefs and sliding them down her legs. She was quivering all over, tiny ripples that were more than skin deep, reaching right inside her, tightening, turning her entire body into a time bomb of need, ready to explode.

She had to hold onto his shoulder to stop herself from losing her balance when he lifted first one small bare foot and then the other clear of her briefs. His skin felt hot and damp, like oiled satin stretched over tough muscle and bone. She dragged in a rough breath and he looked up, his eyes locking with hers, a slash of dull colour highlighting his rugged cheekbones.

They were so close. She was naked. He only had to move his head a fraction and his lips would be touching the soft swell of her tummy. The intimacy, the sexual tension, was pretty close to being unbearable. She swayed slightly towards him in instinctive invitation and heard the inrush of his breath rack through his lungs. Exquisite excitement fizzled through her veins. Surely now...

But he got to his feet, his mouth set in the determined line she knew so well. He led her over to one of the full-length mirrors and swivelled her round to face it, his hands on her shoulders.

'Look at yourself.' His voice was low, terse. 'Tell me what you see.'

Her bewildered gaze met his reflected silver eyes. Uncertainly, she circled her mouth with her tongue, and he said thickly, 'Then I'll tell you. Forget what you were programmed to believe. You're looking at a beautiful woman. You have eyes like pools of liquid gold, a mouth that begs to be kissed, a body to die for—perfectly formed breasts, a tiny waist, flirty hips—' His hands had dropped, long fingers moving to touch the parts of her body he was describing. Mattie felt too giddy to stay upright; blood was rushing ferociously through her veins, pounding in her head.

Self-consciousness dissipated, lost in the red-hot mist of all the things he was doing to her, all the new and wicked sensations he was making her feel. She leaned back against him and he buried his fingers in the mound of her femininity. She sucked in a sharp breath as she instinctively parted her thighs, almost swooning with atavistic desire as his fingers probed more deeply, her hazed eyes watching his reflected hands as they pleasured her body, his head coming down as his mouth found the side of her neck.

And when she felt the potent force of his arousal against her buttocks she squirmed round in his arms, lifting her hips and parting her thighs to accommodate him, all primitive woman meeting her mate.

'Oh, God—Mattie—' Her name was torn from him as he swept her onto the bed, smothering her face, her breasts, with fevered kisses, the silver of his eyes darkened to pewter when he finally positioned himself over her and plunged smoothly into the slick, receptive, willing core of her body. And the rapture came quickly, for both of them, and it was more than she had ever dreamed possible.

There had been no pain, not the slightest hint of it, just ecstasy, a soaring upwards flight to somewhere near the stars and a glimpse of heaven. This first time for her would be something she'd always remember, she thought dreamily, stroking the length of his back as he collapsed on the bed at her side,

gathering her in his arms, tucking her head into the
angle of his shoulder.

'You are incredible.' His voice, husky and deep,
wasn't altogether steady. 'How could you even think
you'd disappoint me when you're so beautiful, so
sexy?'

Mattie murmured incoherently, squirming closer.
In all of her life she'd never been this happy, this
fulfilled. Which made her think.

'James—' She levered herself up on one elbow,
looking down into his adored face, her eyes soft with
love. 'Did you, I mean, have you changed your mind
about having children?' And at the sharp query in
his eyes she explained, 'We didn't take precautions.'

It took a split second for it to sink in. He sat upright, swung his long legs over the edge of the bed.
'Hell, no! Don't get that into your head.' He shot an
unreadable look over his shoulder. 'You made me
lose all control, and, believe me, that was a first.' His
sudden smile was as wicked as sin, sending electri-
fying prickles right through her body. 'You can take
that as a compliment. It should boost your tottery
self-confidence!' He got to his feet, grinning down
at her. 'You're quite something, Matts, do you know
that? You blew away my intention to make your ini-
tiation slow, very thorough and entirely unforgetta-
ble.'

She reached out and took his hand. 'It was unfor-
gettable,' she assured him softly. 'And we've got a
whole month to be as slow and thorough as we want
to be.'

'Correction.' He bent forward to touch her parted
lips with his. 'We have the rest of our lives.' His
eyes suddenly sobered. 'Matts—I'll take precautions

in future—but as for just now, is this a safe time for you? Or should we do something about it?'

He smiled softly at her look of total incomprehension and pulled her up into his arms, his hands locked loosely at her waist. 'This island may be off the beaten track,' he told her, 'but it isn't completely behind the times. There's a pharmacy—we could get a morning-after pill.'

'No.' She felt her body stiffen with rejection. His suggestion might be practical but it wasn't romantic. And she was determined to keep romance high on her agenda. Besides, she was hardly likely to get pregnant from making love just once. It took some couples years of trying before they were able to make a baby! 'No, no need,' she told him firmly. 'It's perfectly safe.' For all she knew it was—how was she to know where the so-called safe time in her cycle came? She'd never thought about it, never had the need to.

But she felt a niggling twinge of guilt when he took her at her word. 'If you say so, sweetheart, it's good enough for me! Now, I guess we should shower and dress, otherwise we're going to keep Mercy and her lunch waiting. Though, right now, eating's the last thing on my mind. Coming?'

'Be right with you.' She wasn't hungry for food, either. But as they'd suggested lunch at one it would be unforgivably rude if they failed to turn up. Following him through to the bathroom, she had a tiny flicker of sadness at the thought of never bearing a child of his. But he was so obviously and adamantly against starting a family. And if it came down to a choice between having him as her husband and having a whole brood of children by any other man on the planet, she'd choose him.

Every time.

CHAPTER EIGHT

'DO WE really have to go to this thing tonight?' Mattie asked.

She sounded slightly tense, James thought. She hadn't sounded like that for months—not since they had been together on the island, anyway. So why this evening?

He closed the bedroom door behind him and started to unknot his tie. The warm glow that crept around his heart whenever he saw her was such a regular occurrence that he didn't think about it, he just accepted it as part of their satisfactory life together.

'Afraid so,' he answered, brushing her cheek with the customary 'Nice To See You Again' kiss. Clad in a black silk slip, she looked delectable. As always, whatever she happened to be wearing. He tossed his tie onto the huge double bed they now shared with such enthusiasm. His suit jacket followed.

'It's one of the biggest charity thrashes in London and I'm on the committee, as you know.' He unbuttoned his shirt and removed his trousers. 'We have to put in an appearance.'

Puzzled, he noted the slight droop of her mouth as she sat in front of the mirror and reached for a pot of something or other. It wasn't like Mattie to baulk at a cocktail do, something that would merely involve circulating for half an hour or so clutching a glass of wine, making small talk.

Socially, she had blossomed out of all recognition. The quiet academic who had never been happier than when shut away with her work had been consigned to the past, happily consigned on her part, he was sure of that.

His wife of three months—he didn't count the couple of months or whatever when they'd been living a sham—had excelled in becoming the best hostess in London.

The very best, he thought, admiring the clean lines of her slender naked shoulders.

Naked himself now, ready to take a shower, he went to stand behind her. She'd already had hers. The tendrils of glossy chestnut hair that curved around her jawline were still slightly damp.

He met her eyes in the mirror. Troubled eyes? Surely not. Yet how was he to know? If Mattie had problems she never came to him with them; they didn't have that type of relationship.

No messy emotional scenes of the sort he'd been afraid of when he'd been pussyfooting around the question of whether or not he should tell her he wanted to introduce sex into their marriage. Nothing tortured or angst-ridden to muddy the waters. If Matts had a problem she would simply buckle down and think her way out of whatever it might be.

'Relax,' he said, putting his hands on her shoulders, pushing the narrow straps out of the way as he began to massage the kinks out of tense muscles.

Maybe she was simply tired, and had a long day. 'It will probably bore our socks off, but as long as we show our faces it won't matter if we leave early. We'll have supper in our favourite restaurant after—would you like that?' His hands were caressing now,

sliding forwards, touching the soft warm skin that
rose just above the top of her slip.

'I'm fine, really I am.' Her voice now had a definite husk to it. 'Supper would be lovely.'

The flush that had stolen into her cheeks made her
eyes glitter. There was a tiny zip at the back of her
slip. He pulled it down, eased the cups of the silky
garment out of the way and stroked her breasts.

She was, as always, beautifully responsive. Her
gorgeous breasts were swelling into his hands, her
lips parting, her soft, deliciously scented flesh beginning to quiver, her long, tangled lashes flickering.
Whoever would have guessed that the dowdy ill-
fitting clothes of his little grey Mouse had hidden a
body that was unadulterated, simmering sex? It never
failed to amaze him. Or arouse him.

He shifted closer, pressing against her, his voice
thick, his need great. 'And it won't matter a damn if
we're late.'

'No?' An impish gleam suddenly sparkled in her
reflected eyes. 'You're sure about that?'

'Very.' His breath caught in his lungs as she
twisted round on the stool and every sinew in his
body tightened as he looped his arms around her and
lifted her gently to her feet.

'On your own head be it...' Her voice tailed away
on a breathless whisper, the teasing note swept away
on a rip tide of desire, her mauve-shadowed eyelids
closing as she swayed into the heat of his body and
then away again to step sinuously out of her slip, her
body naked for him except for the wicked black lace
briefs she was wearing.

Waiting for him, wanting him as he wanted her.

Beautiful! His head was swimming, his heart

pounding as he put one hand on her waist, the other at her nape and took her soft, parted lips with his, drowning in her fevered response to his possessive passion, drowning in the sexy grace of her, the sensual loveliness of her, the utter perfection of her.

He gasped as he at last released her mouth, his breath shuddering. 'Witchery... The things you do to me! Sheer witchery—Mattie—!'

His voice didn't sound as if it belonged to him. It sounded as if it came from a man in the throes of a deep and wild emotion. No other woman had ever made him lose his grip.

No other woman—an unheralded thought, as bright as a thread of pure silver, briefly penetrated the fog of desire his brain had become. He tried to grasp it but it slipped away like quicksilver as she insinuated a satin-smooth thigh between his hair-roughened legs and slid her hands down over his stomach to cradle the potent force of his manhood, the movements so erotic it made his bones shake.

With a muffled groan he swept her up into his arms and carried her to the bed. And kissed her, kissed every silken, scented inch of her skin, sliding the wicked briefs down the length of her lovely legs, taking his time, making this right, needing to give her everything of himself, to make it as perfect for her as she made it for him.

Her breathing was shallow and fast, her hands touching him, demanding, feverish, her body on fire, burning for his, and he knew her so well, knew every nuance of expression, knew, quite exactly, when to cover her, to slide deep within her, feeling her buck against him, her body arching with need, and when she cried his name hoarsely and he felt her body spasm around him he let himself go and was consumed in the liquid, golden fire that was his Mattie.

His Mattie. His wife. The woman who had come into his life, made magic, transformed it. Made changes in him he was only just beginning to properly understand, to welcome.

They were very late, Mattie thought, looking around. The venue was packed with the seriously rich and the type of people who hung around them. The noise level was absolutely incredible.

'I don't want to leave you,' James said, taking two glasses of what looked suspiciously like flat champagne from one of the circulating waiters. 'You look so beautiful. But needs must. We'll circulate and I'll meet you back here in thirty minutes. No more. Then I'll wine and dine you, and after that, who knows?'

His eyes had the drenched look they always had after they'd made love, Mattie thought, watching him swing away into the throng. Not only once, on the bed, but again in the shower. They couldn't keep their hands off each other. But beautiful? Well, she did her best. The tawny russet-coloured sleeveless silk sheath she was wearing was one of the 'Must Haves' Dawn had insisted she buy all those months ago.

Soon she wouldn't be able to get into it.

Which was why she hadn't wanted to come here tonight. She needed to tell him she was pregnant.

Her GP had confirmed it this morning. Three months pregnant. It must have been that very first time in Barbados. The only time they'd made love without using protection. And she'd assured him there would be no consequences and, worse, he'd trusted her implicitly. It made her feel just awful!

She didn't know how he was going to take the news. It was something she was going to have to find out, and sooner rather than later.

He didn't want children. And she didn't want the child she was carrying to be unwanted by its father.

Already she was feeling fiercely protective of the new life inside her.

But surely, once he got used to the idea of father-hood, he'd be happy, too. She knew why he was so adamantly against having a family of their own. It went back to his childhood. He was afraid that he, like his own parents, would be unable to commit to a child, and he wouldn't condemn any child to the type of upbringing he had had.

However, she consoled herself as she offloaded her untouched drink onto a passing waiter, she knew him better than he knew himself. He was kind and caring and wouldn't knowingly harm another living crea-ture. He was capable of love.

He hadn't learned to love her, of course, she knew that. He liked her, respected her, and he enjoyed hav-ing sex with her. But she didn't touch his emotions; her female instincts, so finely tuned into him, would have told her if she had.

But it would be different with his child. Of course he would love it. Wouldn't he?

She edged around the knot of people directly in front of her, smiling indiscriminately at those she knew and those she didn't know from Adam, and looked around for James. Another twenty minutes or so and they'd be out of here. She'd break the news over supper. He'd be relaxed and—hopefully—receptive.

'All alone and no one to play with? What a shame!'

Mattie would have recognised that cut-glass accent anywhere. Forcing herself not to cringe, she turned round slowly and put an empty smile on her face.

'Fiona.'

'As ever. James deserted you, has he? Again.'

Mattie refused to let herself rise to the bait. The wretched woman couldn't have heard of James' prolonged absence in Spain so soon after their marriage. Could she? Besides, they'd been together since that idyllic month on the island, a loving couple. Well, she amended silently, loving on her part.

'Just making the rounds, doing his duty,' she said airily. But Fiona ignored that, sweeping her eyes from the crown of Mattie's glossy chestnut head down to her bronze-toned high-heeled slippers.

'Nice try in the transformation department, sweetie, but not good enough. Nowhere near good enough to hold onto a man like James. He insists on style where his women are concerned. As I should know.'

Mattie resisted the urge to reach out and slap that lovely but supercilious face. Fiona might sound as if she came out of the top drawer, which she did, sound as if she had a silver spoon in her mouth which, if rumour was right, she didn't because all the crested family silver had been sold off years ago, but the dress she was almost wearing said something entirely different. Something like tarty. Too low, too short, too tight.

Fiona was a bitch. For some reason she hadn't

wanted to marry James herself, but she couldn't stand to see him with someone else. Mattie wasn't prepared to stand here and take her spiteful put-downs.

'Style?' she questioned with a sweet smile. 'You misuse the word, if you're referring to yourself. The words blatant and obvious spring more aptly to mind.'

That got to Fiona, it really did, the veneer of sophistication blown away on a blast of temper. The biter wasn't at all happy about being bit! The cold eyes narrowed and the scarlet mouth spat. 'You know nothing! It wasn't you he wanted, it was me. Always me! He was gutted when I broke our engagement. And do you know why I did? No? Then I'll tell you. He said he didn't want children. Ever. He even threatened that if I got "accidentally" pregnant he'd leave me to bring it up on my own. On that subject there was no room for manoeuvre. So I called the wedding off.'

The rush of satisfaction Mattie had experienced when she'd stood up for herself drained away. She felt sick. Fiona didn't look the maternal type, but then, what did she know? About anything?

What the other woman had said rang horribly true. It didn't augur well for her own situation.

'However—' the cut-glass tones lowered an octave, sensing victory '—I've had time to reconsider. I'm still as crazy about him as he is about me. And as soon as he knows I've changed my mind, that I don't mind being childless if that's what he wants, he'll dump you because all you ever were to him was a poor second best. And if you don't believe it, just watch me. I'll prove it to you.'

And she did. It was incredible, but she did just that.

But it wasn't really incredible at all, Mattie thought despairingly, finding a wall to lean against. Hadn't she always suspected that James hadn't got over losing the only woman out of the dozens that had gone before that he'd wanted as his wife?

She'd hoped that time and the obvious pleasure he took in their lovemaking would make him forget, that eventually he'd grow to love her.

But, watching the two of them together, she knew it wasn't going to happen.

Fiona must have intercepted him on his way to collect her. And now the two of them were standing close together, very close, absorbed in each other. For them, it seemed, no one else existed in this crowded room.

His dark head was bent to hear what she was saying. He looked happy, his mouth softened into the curve of sensuality she recognised so well. It was the look he wore when he was making love to her.

Only he hadn't been making love to her, had he? With his body, perhaps, but not with his heart or his head. In his mind he would have been imagining he was with Fiona, his real and only love. That was the hardest thing of all to bear.

She saw Fiona lift her hand, place her fingers against his mouth, saw him take that hand in his and then someone blocked her view, speaking to her, putting a glass of something into her hand.

Mattie tried to pull herself out of her nightmare but could only nod now and then and hope that would pass for polite social intercourse. She vaguely recognised the middle-aged male face but couldn't put a name to it. He was talking about some dinner party or other, mentioning other guests, so they must have met there. She wished he would go away.

'Evening, Lester, I'm afraid I'm going to have to break this up.' Suddenly, James' hand was cupping her elbow. Mattie shuddered. He took the untouched drink out of her hand and disposed of it. 'A supper engagement, you know how it is.'

He looked so happy it hurt her. Because of what Fiona had been saying? The other woman had given her fair warning, after all. She looked away from him, knowing she had to harden her heart, stop feeling anything for him.

It was still light outside, a lovely June evening. James hailed a cruising cab. Mattie said, 'I don't want supper. I'd prefer to go straight home.'

'Why? Is something wrong?' He looked disappointed, she conceded. Because, after his intimate tête-à-tête with the love of his life, he had been looking forward to telling her, the stand-in, to hop it, softening her up with good food and lashings of wine first. As she herself had planned on doing before she broke her own news.

'I'm too tired,' she said, diving into the back of the taxi. Time enough to tell him exactly what was wrong when they were guaranteed some privacy. She was pregnant, that was what was wrong. If he'd threatened Fiona with instant desertion if she 'accidentally' fell pregnant, what chance did she have of his support?

None whatsoever. She hadn't realised his anti-children feelings were so deep, so strong. He was damaged material.

Yet she still loved him.

No, she didn't, she came back at herself, desperately trying to harden a heart that already felt as if it had been put through a mincer, all small, broken, quivery pieces. She squeezed herself up into the far corner as he joined her after giving the driver their Belgravia address. And he did look concerned, his brows meeting, his mouth a straight line as he said, 'If you're feeling unwell, tell me.'

Concern? Hardly. She was misreading him. He was simply puzzled, even annoyed. He expected compliance from her, an easy passage, no female mood swings, no hassle. Sex on tap. Just sex, with no messy emotions attached. And up until now that had been exactly what he had got.

'I'm not ill,' she said through her teeth. 'Just tired, as I told you.' Tired of being second best, tired of loving with no hope of it ever being returned. And an impulse she couldn't quell made her add, 'Did you have a nice chat with Fiona? I thought she looked particularly—spectacular—this evening!'

She wasn't going to say she looked like a strumpet out on the pull! She wouldn't demean herself by letting her jealousy show through. She did have some pride.

'Ah.' Just a small sound, but it said it all. He didn't need to elaborate. She'd heard the complacent smile in his voice, felt the release of the tension that had made the air surrounding them feel prickly.

The intimate tête-à-tête she had just reminded him of must have been entirely satisfactory.

The traffic had been relatively light and while he was paying off the driver she let herself into the silent house and went through to the drawing room, the sight of the bowls of flowers that reminded her of their beautiful time in Barbados, the flowers she'd insisted on having here ever since she'd taken over as mistress of his house, irritating her.

They represented the sham her life had become.

Moments later, he followed her. He removed his dark jacket, the soft white fabric of his shirt clinging to the width of his shoulders, tucked into the narrow trousers that clipped his taut waist, skimmed the hard muscles of his thighs.

Mattie closed her eyes. Looking at him hurt her. Would he really wash his hands of her because she'd got pregnant, broken his rules? Even though he was just as much to blame? She recalled the vehemence of his 'Hell, no!' when she'd reminded him that he hadn't taken precautions that first time and rather supposed he would.

After all, she had assured him—believed herself—that there had been little risk of her getting pregnant at that time.

'You're very pale, Matts,' he said, moving closer. 'Would a brandy help?'

She shook her head. She didn't want his polite kindness, his spurious concern. She wanted something real for a change. A true emotion. And that was precisely what she'd get when she broke her news. The way he took it would decide her whole future, and that of their child.

Although, remembering exactly what Fiona had said, she was pretty sure what that future would be.

Suddenly, her legs began to shake. She took a step backwards and sank down onto one of the brocade-covered sofas, her mouth dry as she forced herself to ask, 'When you proposed to Fiona, did you tell her you didn't want children?'

He'd been prowling the room, switching on table lamps, drawing the summer-weight gauzy curtains across the long windows because it was dusky outside now. But he stopped, as if briefly frozen, then slowly turned, his expression quellingly cold.

'As it happens, yes.' His voice was even colder than his narrowed silver eyes. 'Why ask?'

'Because it happens to be important,' she got out with difficulty. She had known Fiona had been telling the truth. It tied in so neatly with everything she knew herself. The only difference being that he hadn't warned her against being sneaky, and accidentally getting pregnant.

Because the marriage wouldn't have been consummated so the situation wouldn't have arisen. Then things had changed and he'd wanted sex. And apart from that first time, when he'd obviously been feeling deprived after a long stretch of celibacy, he'd been meticulous about taking precautions.

She got to her feet. The rest of her life began right here. She had to start the way she meant to go on. With dignity and courage.

'I want a divorce,' she told him, the unexpected steadiness of her voice comforting her a little. She did have the strength to do this; she'd been so afraid she wouldn't, that she'd be weak enough to beg him to let her stay, to love their child even if he couldn't love her.

'I had my pregnancy confirmed this morning,' she told him tonelessly. 'And there's no need to tell me you wash your hands of me because I've broken your precious rules, because tomorrow I'm leaving you. There's no way I want my child to have anything to do with a father who doesn't want it, someone as sick, bitter and twisted as you seem to be.' She walked to the door. 'I'll use one of the spare rooms tonight, and I'd appreciate it if you didn't bring Fiona here until after I've gone.'

She turned to look at him for one last time. She didn't know what would happen if he asked her not to go. In all probability she'd cave in. But he didn't. His features might have been carved from stone, his eyes just as hard.

He was letting her go without a single word. At that moment she hated him almost as much as she had ever loved him.

She walked out, closing the door quietly behind her.

There was no need for him to say anything, not when she'd just done his dirty work for him.

CHAPTER NINE

ON HER way upstairs to make up a bed in one of the spare rooms, Mattie changed her mind.

Why wait until morning? If she was leaving she might just as well do it now. James wasn't exactly pounding up the stairs after her, pleading with her to stay. The formality of divorce aside, their marriage was over.

In fact, the silence of his complete indifference was deafening.

Mrs Briggs would be around in the morning, serving breakfast, asking who would be in for lunch and who wouldn't. Mattie could do without having to tell her that she didn't want breakfast, wouldn't be eating another meal in this house. Ever.

Thankfully, there was no large-scale business entertaining in the offing to worry the elderly housekeeper. And when there was, Fiona would be only too happy to do the organising, she thought sourly.

In the room she had shared with James she pushed as many of her belongings as she could manage to get into an overnight bag. The rest could stay here and rot for all she cared.

After hurriedly checking the contents of her handbag, she crept back down the stairs feeling like a thief and was on the pavement a scant five minutes after walking out on James. But her feet felt rooted to the spot, as if the physical effort entailed in walking out of his life was beyond her.

She was still actually waiting for him to come after her, she thought with a shock of self-disgust. To beg her to stay, tell her he couldn't live without her, that he'd changed his mind about having a family.

Waiting for something that would never happen.

Tugging in a harsh breath, she forced herself to walk on, wishing she'd had the sense to change out of the spindly high heels, no idea where she was going.

James had never pretended he loved her. Why should he, when he didn't, when all she was to him was a pleasant, undemanding companion, someone to share his bed and satisfy strong male urges?

He'd said nothing when she'd dropped her bombshell, just stared at her, his features frozen, not even bothering to call her back when she'd walked out of the room.

After his conversation with Fiona this evening he would have been relieved to see her go. Her and the child she was carrying, the child he most definitely didn't want.

It was almost dark now, the June night warm, the traffic light. She simply walked, not seeing anything, her mind replaying nightmare scenes from this evening.

Without any conscious mental direction she found herself in front of the apartment block where her father lived with his new wife.

Somewhere to spend the night, she thought dully when she recognised where she was. In the absence of a mother, she was running home to Father, instinctively trying to burrow back into the womblike existence she'd known before she'd accepted James' proposal.

When her father opened the door he was wearing a thin robe over his stripy pyjamas, sloppy old slippers on his feet. And a puzzled expression on his face.

'Can I stay the night?' Her voice sounded rusty, as though she hadn't used it for years. She walked stiffly past him, holding herself rigid because if she didn't she could easily fall apart, walked through the pleasant square-shaped entrance hall, into the long, rectangular sitting room. Pleasant, too, decorated in soft shades of sage-green and lighter touches of ivory, furnished with comfortable pieces brought from Berrington.

She'd visited before, of course she had. But never dressed for a cocktail party, a bulging old canvas holdall hitched over one shoulder, her handbag over the other, her face stiff with the dried runnels of tears she hadn't known she'd shed.

'Of course you can stay.' Edward Trent had followed his daughter, but slowly, as if he were negotiating a minefield. 'You can stay for as long as you like. But may I be allowed to know why?'

She turned to face him, letting the bags she was carrying slip to the floor. 'I've left James.' Saying it aloud made the muddled nightmare of this evening real. Gave it a sharpness and clarity that hurt unbearably. She dragged her hand over her eyes. 'It didn't work out. It was never going to.' How could it have done when he couldn't stop loving Fiona?

'Why don't you sit down before you keel over?' Edward suggested worriedly. 'Can I get you something to drink? Coffee, or would you like something stronger?'

She ignored his question, as if she hadn't taken it

in, her eyes looking bruised as she scanned the room. 'Where's Emily?' She'd known and liked her new stepmother for what felt like for ever. Over the years she'd taken the place of the mother who had deserted her. In the midst of the emotional storm that was engulfing her she craved the comfort of the familiar.

But her father said, 'She turned in early. We planned on driving up to York tomorrow. Staying a few days and taking in the sights. But that can be postponed, it's not important. What appears to be happening with you is.'

'No.' Abruptly, with all the determination she possessed, she pulled herself together. What right had she to inflict her miseries and messes on her father and his new wife? She wouldn't disrupt their lives with her problems. She could handle them herself.

'Just tonight,' she assured him, more life in her voice now. 'I'll be leaving London tomorrow, too. I'd hate you to change your plans on my account. Besides, there wouldn't be any point. Tea,' she said, lifting her chin. 'I'd like a cup, would you?'

She walked through to the clinically perfect kitchen without waiting for his reply. She felt strangely calm now, almost as if nothing could touch her, as if she were living inside a glass bubble where she was safely beyond reach of anything that could hurt her.

After filling the kettle she plugged it in and her father said uncomfortably, from just behind her, 'You don't have to tell me what's gone wrong if you don't want to. And it may seem a silly question, knowing James as well as I do, but has he hurt you? Been unkind?'

'No.' Her voice was flat. Her father meant hurt in

the physical sense. And yes, that was a silly question because James wasn't the violent type, except where the passionate depth of his emotions regarding Fiona were concerned.

And was it 'unkind' to be unable to love someone? She didn't somehow think so. He couldn't help not loving her, loving Fiona instead. Love made you blind to everything, love made the beloved the focus of your entire existence, the rest of the world peopled by cardboard cut-outs, having no real relevance.

As she knew from her own bitter experience.

'It's just not working out,' she offered, to soften the bleak monosyllable. 'And you really mustn't worry about it, or me, or let it affect the good relationship you have with James.'

She spooned loose leaves from the caddy into the teapot and lined up two cups and saucers on the work surface, reaching the milk jug from the fridge, her movements smoothly automatic. It was remarkable, really, the adult way she was handling this, she thought objectively. She felt vaguely detached, as if she were watching someone else go through the motions, listening to another woman talk such sound, good sense.

The tea made, poured, Edward took his cup to the table and sat down heavily. Mattie joined him and he asked, 'Where will you go? What will you do?'

'The agency will find me enough to do, I can work from anywhere, you know that. And as for where—' she shrugged her slight shoulders '—I'll let you know when I know myself.'

'You'll need help,' Edward said decisively. 'Emily and I will be only too glad—'

'No,' Mattie said again. She had to stand on her

own feet—she needed to if she were to come out of this with her self-respect intact. She had to order her own life, her own future. 'Financially, I'm fine, as you know. Hopefully, I'll find somewhere I like to rent fairly soon. I'll keep in close touch and, as I've already told you, you really mustn't worry about me.'

'How can I help it?' Edward grimaced. 'I admit, I did have a few private doubts about your marriage at first, coming so soon after that Fiona whats-her-name fiasco, and James' unnecessarily prolonged absence in Spain. But when you came back from that delayed honeymoon I knew everything was OK. James had lost some of those sharp edges of his and I've never seen you look so radiant.'

He took her hands across the table and held them tightly. 'And now you seem set on throwing it all away. Mattie—' he dragged in a huff of breath '—all marriages go through bad patches. The thing is, you stay right with it, you don't just walk out on something that's basically good, you work to get it back on track. Why don't you go back tomorrow, sit down with James and talk? Try to sort out whatever problem you have? I dare say you don't think much of that idea right now, but will you at least promise to think about it?'

Gently, she extricated her fingers from his fierce grasp. She stood up. He looked so concerned. She really shouldn't have come here and dumped this on him. 'I'll think about it,' she promised.

If she thought about it for ever, it wouldn't make a scrap of difference, the circumstances wouldn't change, but he wouldn't know that. At least she'd been guarded enough not to blurt out the truth of the situation.

She managed a weary smile. 'I will think it over, but only if you promise me something in return.'

'And that is?'

He looked brighter now, a touch of relief in his answering smile. Mattie breathed more easily. She loved her father and hated the thought of worrying him. 'That you and Emily take off, as planned, to-morrow, and forget my problems. They'll get sorted, one way or another.' She managed a small smile. 'I know you think I'm hopeless when it comes to any-thing calling for common sense, but, believe me, I've changed. Now, when are you due back here?'

'Next Friday, at the latest.'

'Then I'll phone that evening. OK?'

'Right.' Edward got to his feet. 'Time we both got some sleep. And remember your promise—you think long and hard before you do anything drastic.'

Mattie kept her promise. It didn't do any harm to think about seeing James, sitting down with him and talking things over. But that was as far as it would go. Translating thought into action would be a waste of time. The truth was the truth and nothing could change it.

She fell into a troubled sleep at dawn and woke again when she heard her father and Emily moving around. Six o'clock and the promise of another hot summer day.

Suddenly remembering the look of worried con-cern on her father's face the night before, she slith-ered out of bed and stumbled into the guest room's *en suite*. By now Emily would have been told what was happening and she'd be worried, too. She,

Mattie, was in danger of wrecking their jaunt to historic York.

It simply wouldn't do. She was loved by both of them, she knew that, but it didn't give her the right to heap her problems on their heads.

She showered quickly and towelled her face violently to put some colour in it. In her emotional haste to leave she'd left her make-up behind.

Emotional haste?

Pulling garments out of the holdall, she paused, recalling everything she'd said to James the evening before. Had she overreacted, spoken wildly, because her hormones were all over the place? She'd heard, or read somewhere, that pregnancy could play havoc with a woman's equilibrium. Certainly, the way she'd acted had been totally out of character.

Thoughtfully, she pulled on a pair of white cotton jeans, tucking a sleeveless, lemon yellow blouse into the waistband. Some of the things she'd said to him made her feel ashamed of herself.

Besides, what had happened had been as much her fault as his. She should never have accepted his proposal in the first place and she certainly shouldn't have allowed him to use her to slake his desire for sex. Loving him for so long had robbed her of all her common sense, made her believe that one day he would love her too.

Pushing her feet into flat leather sandals, she pinched some more colour into her cheeks, straightened her shoulders and walked through the apartment to the kitchen.

Her father and Emily, still in their dressing gowns, were sitting at the table, the teapot and cups in front of them.

Mattie pulled in a sharp breath, remembering the day they'd been married. Emily had looked lovely, her father so proud and content. They were making a good life together, she wasn't going to spoil it for them.

She could tell them the truth about her marriage of convenience, of course, and they would understand, be on her side. And worry even more. Best to say nothing about that, let them know what had really happened, bit by bit, when they knew she was settled somewhere, and coping.

'Mattie—oh, my dear!' Emily rose immediately and folded her arms comfortingly around her. 'Edward told me. Now what can we do to help?'

'Nothing,' Mattie said as lightly as she could, returning her stepmother's hug. 'Except get ready for your trip while I make breakfast.'

'We couldn't possibly!' Emily held her at arm's length, concerned eyes searching her face. 'Not while you're in such trouble.'

'Yes, you could,' Mattie said firmly. 'I feel a whole lot calmer this morning. I shouldn't have come here. I should have gone to an hotel and got my head straight there, not come whingeing to you!'

'You do look better,' Edward said uncertainly. 'Can I take it you kept your promise and thought about talking things out with James?'

'Yes. I'll go home after you leave—remember the promise you made me? It's Sunday, so he won't be at the office.' Subconsciously, she must have made the decision while she'd been dressing. She couldn't leave him like this, not having given him the opportunity to tell her his side of the story, draw a firm line beneath the end of their relationship.

And she hadn't told him she would expect nothing in the way of a divorce settlement, or that she wouldn't expect him to pay for the maintenance of a child he didn't want. That she could cope as a single mother more than adequately on her own. Tell him that if he ever wanted to know the sex of their child, ever wanted to see it, claim his visiting rights, then he would only have to ask. He probably wouldn't, but the offer would be there.

She'd apologise, too, for the things she'd said. Telling him he was sick, bitter and twisted had been well out of order. Above everything else, they'd always been friends. Their marriage may have been doomed from the start, but she didn't want it to end in hatred and bitterness.

'Well—' Edward glanced at his wife '—I did promise. And you're sure you're going to sit down with James and talk, sensibly?'

'Quite sure. Now will you two please go and get dressed?'

They went, but with a marked reluctance. Mattie told herself she had to try harder in the reassurance department. She made fresh tea, scrambled eggs and toasted bread, more and more convinced that seeing James again was the only right thing to do. That they should part amicably was now desperately important to her.

She wouldn't let herself think that he might ask her to stay, tell her he wanted their baby, that he didn't want to put Fiona in her place.

She was realistic enough to recognise that allowing herself to hope for that would only lead to further heartbreak.

*   *   *

The ten-minute walk seemed to take for ever. She tried to hurry but her legs wouldn't go any faster. What if he'd been so unperturbed by her self-admittedly manic departure that he'd decided to put in a few hours at the office, undisturbed by telephones or faxes?

And thinking of telephones, why hadn't he called her? He must have guessed that after hurtling out last night she would have gone to her father's apartment. He hadn't bothered to phone and check.

Even if he'd taken her statement that she'd sleep in one of the spare rooms at face value, and hadn't bothered to even look in on her, to attempt to talk things over, by this time he would have realised she wasn't in the house this morning.

It had been gone ten before her father and step-mother had finally started out, and at least another half an hour had passed while she'd stripped the bed she'd used, tidied up, getting herself calm enough to face him, to say goodbye properly to the only man she had ever loved, to apologise unreservedly for the bad things she'd said about him.

But that was what she'd come here to put right, wasn't it? she told herself when she finally stood before his elegant front door.

She hadn't kept her door key. Steeling herself, trying to subdue her jangling, dancing nerve-ends, she pressed the polished brass bell, hoping Mrs Briggs was somewhere deep inside the house and James would answer it himself.

Turning her back on the solid door, she wiped her damp palms down the sides of her jeans and tried to relax her tense shoulder muscles.

Dammit, even her teeth were chattering! And no

matter how hard she tried, she couldn't stop the totally irrational hope that, somehow, a miracle would happen, and everything would be all right.

The door was opened. Mattie heard it and tried to get the bones in her legs to remember that they weren't made of jelly. She forced a smile to her lips and felt it wobble alarmingly as she turned, then fall away completely as she confronted Fiona.

Who said, 'What do you want?'

Mattie couldn't breathe, the pain around her heart was too intense.

He'd moved Fiona in already!

She blinked, her throat going dry. Hadn't the foul woman said that he'd lose no time in installing her, having her in his life, in his bed, because they were still crazy about each other?

And she was looking eye-poppingly sexy. A tiny scarlet skirt revealed the perfection of her endless legs and the skinny-rib cotton vest she was wearing did nothing to disguise the fact that her magnificent breasts were bra-less.

Mattie tried to speak, to ask to see her husband, to make some attempt to push past the other woman, to go inside and find him, but couldn't.

'Look, don't stand there like a dummy,' Fiona said with hasty impatience. 'Didn't I tell you he'd get rid of you as soon as I said the word? He said you might come crawling back, and if you did I was to tell you his solicitor will contact yours. You're not wanted around here. So just go, will you?'

The door was closed decisively in her face.

Slowly, Mattie turned and stumbled away, her body filled with pain. There was nothing for her here. Nothing left of her brief marriage, not even friendship. Certainly not caring. James didn't care what became of her and their child.

She would never have imagined that the man she'd known and loved for so many years could be so callous.

She had never really known him at all.

CHAPTER TEN

Six months later

MATTIE sat on the side of the hospital bed, a warm coat over the maternity dress she'd arrived in. Any time now her father and Emily would collect her from the private room they'd insisted she have.

She couldn't wait to take her baby daughter out of the hospital atmosphere and back to their cosy cottage; she couldn't wait to show her her home.

Her smile loving, she gently eased away the soft folds of the woollen shawl that made a small bundle in her arms and ate up the tiny pink face with her eyes.

'You're a Christmas child,' she said softly. 'So how do you like the name Noelle? Oh, I see, not a lot!' Her smile broadened to an infatuated grin as the blue eyes batted open then screwed shut again, the rosebud mouth blowing a raspberry. 'You think it's far too obvious? And it isn't Christmas Day until tomorrow. Ok, forget Noelle. How about Chloe? That's pretty, don't you think? And do you know something? When I was small I always felt sorry for kids who had birthdays and Christmases close together. I don't see why you shouldn't have two birthdays—a real one and an official one, like the Queen.'

The baby slept. Mattie dropped a feather-light kiss

141

on the tiny forehead. Forty-eight hours old and there was already a strong resemblance to her father.

James. During the months since that fateful evening back in June she'd been successful in knocking any thoughts of him right out of her mind the very moment they'd intruded. It had been the only way.

As soon as she'd got settled she'd told her father what had happened. She was pregnant. James didn't want children. James still wanted Fiona. End of story. She'd made him promise that he wouldn't, in any circumstances, let James know where she was—not that she thought he would ask—but it was best to make sure.

Any necessary contact could be made through their solicitors, she had echoed the message he'd had Fiona pass on. And after that she'd refused to have his name mentioned during their regular phone calls and their occasional visits.

But strangely enough, from the moment when she'd first held her daughter in her arms, thoughts of James had come thick and fast, unhindered by her strict mental censor. Mostly they'd been of pity. He would never know the sheer joy of holding a child of his in his arms, never know the purity of completely selfless love or this fiercely protective pride.

And just sometimes there was a deep and aching sense of regret…

Frowning softly, she glanced up at the round face of the wall clock, then relaxed. In her eagerness to get home she'd got dressed and ready far too early. Her father and Emily would be here within the next five minutes.

'Ten o'clock in the morning, on the dot,' Emily had promised as they'd left after visiting the evening before. 'The nursery's warmed and aired—that night storage heater you had installed works a treat—and there'll be a fire in the sitting room, and Edward went shopping for the turkey and trimmings. So we can all have a lovely relaxed Christmas.'

They'd been so good to her, Mattie thought, insisting on spending the last month of her pregnancy at the cottage, making sure she didn't do too much, that she ate properly, that they were on hand to drive her to the hospital in Dorchester when she went into labour.

She could have managed on her own, of course, but it was nice to feel cosseted and pampered for a change. And Christmas was a time for families. Her father, Emily and baby Chloe, what more could she want?

James.

His name came unbidden, unwanted. She clamped her suddenly trembling lips together. It was only to be expected, she excused her wayward thoughts swiftly. Chloe was his baby, too. And a mere forty-eight hours after giving birth it was only natural that she should be feeling vulnerable, her thoughts constantly flying to the man who had created the miracle of this new and precious life with her.

She would soon get back on track. No problem. Once back in her rented cottage on the outskirts of the Dorset village she had fallen in love with over the last few months, she'd be fine. Absolutely one hundred per cent fine.

Her soft mouth relaxed a little; already she was feeling far more positive. Giving herself a sensible talking to was all it took. But her heart took a negative nosedive when James walked into the room, closely followed by one of the pretty young nurses.

For a moment she thought she was seeing things, that her mind was playing tricks on her. Her heart seemed to stop, then thundered on as if it were trying to shake her body to pieces.

His thick dark hair and his black leather jacket were spangled with moisture and the austerity which had been softened during that brief time when she'd believed they'd been happy together was back with a vengeance.

The slightly hooded eyes were grim as they fastened on her and the baby. Mattie shuddered. He looked as if he hated the sight of both of them!

'Your husband was able to collect you and baby after all, Mrs Carter. Isn't that great?' the young nurse burbled.

Mattie thought, Not great at all. Shocking, scary, completely bewildering fitted the bill far better.

But she couldn't say anything, not in front of an audience. She couldn't tell him to go away, to leave her and the baby alone, remind him that he didn't want either of them.

And the nurse was dimpling under the force of that the-man-can't-help-it seductive smile of his as he turned to her. 'We'd better make it snappy. It's snowing like it means it out there.'

Mattie stumbled to her feet as the nurse was chattering happily about the prospect of a white Christmas. She felt as if she were floating, her legs turned to rubber, only able to stay upright because of the precious bundle she was holding.

After passing Mattie's small suitcase to James the nurse stopped commenting on the weather, smiled down into the sleeping baby's face, something James had noticeably neglected to do, and asked brightly, 'Have you decided on a name yet?'

'Chloe,' Mattie answered decisively, shooting a defiant look at James as she felt the strength flow back through her body. The baby was his, but that didn't give him any right at all to interfere in any aspect of their lives, and she would tell him as much as soon as they got rid of their audience of one.

Who was saying, 'Now remember to get as much rest as you can for the next few weeks, Mrs Carter. And if you're at all worried about little Chloe don't hesitate to phone your midwife. She'll be calling on you soon, in any case.'

Her words buzzed into Mattie's brain and straight out again and, thankfully, she and James were at last alone in the reception area. Mattie said firmly, 'I don't know what you're doing here.'

'Don't you?' The glance he gave her was without expression, his mouth tight.

'No.' She looked around for a seat but they all seemed to be occupied. 'You've wasted your time. Dad and Emily are collecting us.'

'They should be well on their way back to London by now,' he replied tersely. 'I'm here to take you home.'

Mattie's eyes glittered with stinging tears and her stomach tightened painfully. They'd abandoned her! Oh, how could they? And why on earth did he want to take her home? That Fiona wouldn't want to be landed with her lover's wife and newborn baby would be the understatement of the century!

'I am not going back to London with you!' she choked, feeling little Chloe begin to stir in her arms.

Soon she would need feeding again, and changing, and she herself was on the verge of having hysterics. The thought of going to the room she'd just vacated and staying there indefinitely was very tempting.

'I've no intention of dragging you back to London.' He sounded weary. 'We're going to your cottage where, apparently, you are settled and happy. And the sooner you stop arguing, the sooner we'll get there.'

A hand beneath her elbow steered her towards the automatic doors. A frizzle of unwanted sensation ripped through her and she did her best to ignore it, telling herself that if he was wearied by the situation he only had himself to blame.

She hadn't asked him to come. She hadn't wanted him to come. He'd chosen Fiona over her and no longer had any part in her life. Or her baby's.

Yet if things had been different—

No, she would not let her thoughts travel that dangerous road!

The cold air came as a shock after the warmth of the hospital. Chloe stirred again and made a tiny mewing sound, bringing Mattie's protective instincts out, fierce and bristling. He didn't care if his baby was freezing! Apart from that initial encompassing glare he hadn't even bothered to look at his daughter, let alone ask to hold her!

He was callous! Hateful!

'Where's your car?' she snapped out as temper coloured her cheeks. 'My daughter needs to be out of the cold.'

'Calm down,' he advised stonily. 'The Jag's right here.'

It was, too. Half a dozen yards away. It had

stopped snowing now but the sky looked full of it and the ground was white. The pressure of his fingers increased as he guided her to the passenger door, opened it and waited until she had wriggled in before closing it and tossing her suitcase in the boot.

When he joined her she had taken the soft travelling rug she had never known him to carry in his car before and wrapped it around her baby, and as he turned the key in the ignition she commented frostily, 'I suppose my father told you where I was, that my baby had been born.'

Even though she hadn't expected James to bother to ask, she'd made her father promise not to tell him where she was living now. That he had done, probably with the best of intentions, felt like a betrayal.

'Your father kept his word,' he said dryly. 'Emily told me, most likely with Edward's tacit approval. After all, you didn't actually make *her* promise anything. I knew where you were living almost as soon as you knew yourself.'

She flicked a look at the austere perfection of his profile, her voice thready as she stated, 'You knew where I was. But you didn't visit.' That said it all about his total lack of feelings where she was concerned. 'But you came when our baby was born.' That didn't make any kind of sense. A baby was the last thing he wanted.

'I didn't visit because when you didn't reply to either of my letters asking if we could meet on neutral territory to sort things out, you made it plain you didn't want any contact. I presume Edward did pass them on?' He spared her a bitter glance. 'I didn't write directly to your address—you might have taken it into your head to move on, and I knew from Emily that you were happy where you were.'

Mattie bit her tongue, staring straight ahead. Now wasn't the time to tell him she'd burned those two letters unread. It had been very early days, quite soon after she'd settled in. She'd been trying so hard to forget him and his perfidious behaviour, she hadn't been able to handle any type of reminder of him.

Explaining that she'd thrown his letters on the fire would bring forth some scathing, bitter comment from him. She didn't want her baby to pick up any more of these bad vibrations.

They had left the town well behind and were heading into deep country, the lanes narrow and winding. Determined to relax, to stop tension transmitting itself from her to her tiny daughter, she tried to ignore him, imagine he was a complete stranger, a taxi driver maybe, and doggedly concentrated on thinking thoughts of the peaceful and happy variety.

She and Chloe would soon be home. Just the two of them. The doors firmly closed against the elements, the fire burning in the hearth, warm and comfortable.

It wouldn't matter a toss if it was just the two of them; caring for her baby would keep her happy and occupied. And there was lots she could tell her, about the pale lemon and cream nursery that she'd papered and painted herself and decorated with a frieze of teddy bears, about the garden where, next summer, she could sit in her buggy and watch her mother weeding the vegetable patch, tend the hodgepodge of perennials that would transform what had been a jungle of weeds into a perfumed mass of colour, and—

'We're here,' he said.

Mattie blinked, aware she'd been lost in her day-dreams and that reality was now staring her in the face. The Jaguar was drawn up behind her second-hand very ordinary Ford, parked on the clinker drive-way at the side of the thatched cottage.

She moistened her lips. This painful episode would soon be over. 'If you'll pass me my handbag.' It was at her feet. She couldn't reach it without running the risk of squashing her darling baby. 'I'll get my door-key. And thank you,' she said as politely as she could, 'for giving me a lift.' And then more acidly, because she really couldn't help it, 'I won't offer you a cup of tea. I'm sure you want to get back to Fiona as soon as possible.'

He gave her an unreadable look from those black-fringed silver eyes. 'I have the key your father gave me. I stayed here with them last night. I slept in your bed. But I'll use the spare room tonight since they're not here to need it. We have things to sort out, you and I. And I'll be damned if I'm going to let you chicken out of any one of them.'

CHAPTER ELEVEN

MATTIE followed James into the cottage that she'd so painstakingly turned into a home for her and her child. The living room was small, heavily beamed, cosy; the fire Emily had promised and James must have banked up before he'd left to drive to the hospital was burning brightly in the deep stone hearth.

She watched as he removed the fire-guard, stowing it at the side of the inglenook, just as she always did, remove his leather jacket and hang it on the hook on the door that opened onto the twisty wooden staircase.

His presence, as ever, dominated the space and she knew she should feel resentful over the way he appeared to be taking over, regard him as an intruder.

But she couldn't, she thought miserably. His being here felt so right, as if the three of them were a real family. She couldn't handle the feeling because it simply wasn't true.

And she, poor sucker that she was, wanted it to be.

'There really isn't any need for you to stay,' she said croakily. The sooner he was back in London, the sooner she could get back to normal, halt the dangerous regression to the time when they'd been happy, or had seemed to her to be—the time when she'd felt a part of him, had been a part of his life.

'You need looking after.' His reply was terse. 'Sit down, you look like death.'

Did she? And was it any wonder? He had turned up when she'd least expected it, when she'd believed she was well on the way to getting over him. It was like sharing her home with an unexploded bomb.

'You said there were things you wanted to sort out.' She stood her ground. He wanted to talk about the divorce, presumably—she couldn't think of any other reason for the way he'd sought her out. Though why he hadn't gone through their solicitors, as he'd formerly advised, she was too dizzy-brained to fathom.

'They can wait for a day or two, until you're feeling stronger.' His brows were a dark, frowning line. 'That nurse told you to rest up, remember?'

Rest would be impossible while he was here, didn't he know that? Mattie thought wildly. He was filling her space with memories, the impossible yearnings of a heart that had been irrevocably given to the wrong man.

But there was no point in arguing with him, she decided wearily. He was impossibly intractable when it came to getting his own way. Besides, there were too many things to be done.

The baby had worked her arms free of the shawl, her tiny fists punching the air, her rosebud mouth forming the shape of a square. Any moment now she would start bellowing. For such a small scrap of humanity she could make a remarkably loud noise.

'She needs feeding and changing,' Mattie said briskly, maternal instincts immediately taking over. 'Would you hold her for me, please, while I get her things ready?'

She advanced towards him and he retreated, his face shuttered. 'Put her down over there.' His dark

head tipped briefly towards the chintz-covered sofa
Mattie had bought at a house-clearance sale shortly
after she'd moved in here. 'She won't fall off it, not
if you put one of the cushions between her and the
edge.' He backed through the door that led into the
kitchen. 'I'll make you a hot drink.'

Mattie swallowed a spasm of outrage. But for
heaven's sake, what else had she expected? He
couldn't even bring himself to look at his own
daughter, so how could she have imagined he would
hold her?

Carefully, she placed the now red-faced bundle on
the sofa and stripped off her coat, her throat hot and
tight, deploring his cold-hearted attitude towards his
innocent baby.

Nappies and baby wipes were in the suitcase
James had carried in for her and, after calming herself down, she performed the changing operation
without a hitch, more or less.

She was getting the hang of it, Mattie thought,
deliberately blocking James out of her head. She settled herself in a corner of the comfy sofa, undid the
top buttons of her tent-like maternity dress and held
her baby to her breast, her eyes going liquid with
mother love as her tiny daughter suckled greedily.

And they were still glowing as she raised them to
James as he came slowly back into the room, as if
she were inviting him to close the charmed circle of
love, to make it complete.

'Tea.' He put the cup and saucer on a low table
within easy reach. 'There's more in the pot if you
want it.' His voice was bleak as he fetched his jacket,
the expression on his face making her feel utterly
wretched.

The sight of her feeding their baby had filled him with what had to be disgust. She didn't think she could bear it but knew she had to. The man was so anti-children he had even threatened to end his relationship with the only woman he had ever loved if she went against his wishes and fell pregnant.

The sound of the outer door closing behind him was almost a relief. He was leaving. He should never have come. As she heard the Jaguar's engine purr into life tears poured helplessly down her face.

She and her baby filled him with such revulsion he couldn't stand being around them for a moment longer. He had left and she didn't have the remotest idea why he'd come here in the first place.

All she knew was she wished he hadn't. He'd opened up wounds that had at last begun to heal over. The result was more painful than she could have believed possible.

Life had to go on, Mattie told herself as she closed the nursery door on the sleeping infant. For six months she'd known that her future and James' were to run along separate tracks. And she'd got on with it, hadn't she?

There'd been a few minor hiccups, like the time when she'd had to change a fuse and hadn't known how to do it. It had taken her hours of trial and error to manage it. But on the whole she'd surprised herself by her ability to cope with things that had demanded she haul the almost non-existent practical side of her brain into use when it had come to the crunch.

So she would cope again. Put James' brief and unheralded appearance down to one of those brickbats life had the habit of throwing at you from time to time and settle down to healing her battered heart all over again.

This time it would be easier because she had their baby to claim her time and attention, she decided staunchly as she changed into a man-sized sweatshirt and a pair of jogging pants that had that mercy of mercies, an elasticated waist. The huge bump had gone, of course, but as far as her waist was concerned there was still a way to go.

Thankfully James had changed the bedlinen. The duvet cover smelled of the fabric softener she used. She couldn't face the thought of having to wrestle with bedding herself right now and she wouldn't have slept a wink if his tantalising male scent had kept her company.

As it was, the knowledge that he had slept in her room, in her bed, sent prickles tumbling all over her skin and she wouldn't let herself remember what it had been like when they'd shared a bed for so many long, ecstatic nights.

She would not!

Lunch was toast and some pâté she'd found in the well-stocked fridge. She wasn't really hungry but knew she had to eat. She had her daughter to care for and Chloe's welfare was paramount. It would be the worst kind of betrayal if she allowed herself to wallow in self-pity.

At least she wouldn't have to go shopping for supplies for a week or more; her father and Emily had stocked up with enough food to feed a small army. And before then she'd have to work out how to fix the baby seat into the back of her car. It had an alarming number of straps and buckles and the diagrams and instructions that had come with the contraption looked unintelligible to her.

If James had still been here she would have swallowed her pride and asked him to do it for her.

But he wasn't.

The afternoon passed in a hectic round of feeds, nappy changes, de-burping sessions, culminating at teatime with a gentle all-over wash in the plastic bath on the kitchen table and yet another feed.

By five o'clock Mattie was exhausted. Too done in to even think about beginning to cook for herself, she threw a few more logs on the fire, sank into the welcoming depths of the sofa and began to have serious doubts.

Was she really capable of taking on the sole responsibility of caring for this new little life? And what if little Chloe became ill? Would she recognise the difference between a wail of hunger and a cry of pain? Was she fit to be a mother at all?

Exhaustion was clouding her mind, dragging her down. She might have felt more positive if her father and Emily had stayed around as they had said they would, keeping her company, lending a hand.

But she really mustn't blame them. They would have thought they'd been doing the right thing when they'd asked James to collect her, stay with her for a while, fondly imagining that he'd take one look at his baby daughter and be overcome by a rush of sentimentality to the head and that they'd all live happily ever after.

They were normal, good people. They would never imagine that he'd be so revolted by the sight of mother and baby that he'd drive back to London and Fiona as if all the demons in hell were on his tail!

She was too tired to cry, almost too tired to register the sound of the key turning in the lock. She stared at him dully as he walked across the room taking off his coat.

'Sorry to have been so long,' he apologised tightly as he hung the leather jacket on its accustomed peg. 'With the shutters closed you won't have noticed, but it's practically a white-out out there. A couple of times I thought I'd have to abandon the car and walk back.'

'I thought you were on your way back to London,' Mattie said thinly, pulling herself into a more upright position, clasping her hands around her knees.

James bit back an angry expletive. Did she have that much contempt for his character? He pushed his hands through his snow-dampened hair. Now wasn't the time to pick a fight. When she was stronger the truth was going to come out; whatever it took, he'd get it from her. The time for waiting and watching was damn near over, the time for laying his bitter soul bare was almost here.

But right now she looked too frail to take even a breath of contention.

He said, more or less smoothly, 'I had things to do. It took longer than I'd expected, and the road conditions, particularly in the lanes, held me up. Have you eaten?' He changed the subject, firming his mouth when she didn't answer. Her head was bent, her eyes downcast, the flickering firelight making her cheek-bones seem more prominent. Her hair had grown since he'd last seen her. It was scraped back into a kind of band. If it was loose, he guessed, it would reach her shoulders. She looked achingly vulnerable. 'Then I'll fix something for both of us,' he said tightly, swung round on his heels, headed for the kitchen, then turned back.

Something was missing. For once she wasn't clutching her baby with the fierceness of a mother tiger with her cub. 'Is the child asleep?'

Mattie nodded, her teeth worrying at her lower lip. At least 'the child' was better than 'it'. Marginally.

'Will you hear her if she wakes?'

She ignored the brusqueness of his tone. It wasn't important. Her heart gave a small jerk of pleasure. He was capable of concern for his tiny daughter, even though he hadn't been able to look at her properly and had refused to hold her.

Her features relaxed slightly as she indicated the baby listener beside her on the sofa. 'I have this. I'll hear her as soon as she wakes.'

'Right.'

He disappeared into the kitchen and Mattie sagged back into the corner of the sofa. Relief that he was here, that he hadn't deserted her was warring with the certainty that she was better off without him. The emotional battle was wearing her down.

But by the time he called her into the kitchen she had let it go. She was simply too tired to do anything other than go with the flow—wherever it took her.

The oil-fired Rayburn gave out a comfortable warmth, bunches of dried herbs hung from the chunky overhead beams and the square pine table was laid for supper. It was all so dear and familiar to her it brought weak tears to her eyes.

James should have looked glaringly out of place.

But he didn't. In fact, when he handed her a plate of grilled fillet steak he looked like the most comforting thing she'd ever set eyes on.

He'd grilled mushrooms and tomatoes, too, and made a green salad. 'Eat,' he instructed, pouring red wine for them both. 'Then bed. You need an early night. I'll see to the clearing up.'

Stupid tears misted her eyes and her mouth quivered as she cut into the tender meat. She was grateful that he appeared to have put the discussion about their pending divorce on hold. She couldn't have faced it. Tomorrow, maybe, she'd be feeling strong enough.

She ate as much as she could manage, drank a little of the wine, and wondered if he could tell how badly her eyelids were drooping. In the background she could hear the washing machine chugging through its cycle in the lean-to utility room. For the first time she noticed that the bundle of baby laundry she'd left on the floor, intending to put it through the machine later, was missing.

He was a rock she wanted to cling to and any time now she'd find herself down on her knees, thanking him for being here for her. She couldn't let that happen. She had to get a grip.

'Thank you.' Mattie put her cutlery down. She wasn't going to express her surprise that he could cook a mean steak and go on to remind him that they'd learned rudimentary cooking skills together last Christmas. It was better to keep away from anything personal. She pushed herself to her feet. Every muscle in her body was aching with fatigue. 'I'll take your advice and turn in now.'

*   *   *

Somehow she made it up the stairs without falling asleep and when she finally crawled beneath the duvet she went under instantly. To be woken some time later by the wail of a hungry baby.

Gaining consciousness as quickly as she'd lost it, she rolled out of bed and stumbled to the small nursery at the head of the staircase, falling over her feet, pushing her hair out of her eyes with one hand, feeling for the door knob with the other.

'Coming, sweetheart,' she croaked. 'Hang on in there. We'll have you dry and comfy in no time.' By the dim night light she assembled everything she needed. Changing mat, clean nappy, baby wipes, cream. A fresh body suit.

Broken nights would be the norm for some time to come, she thought without rancour as she sank into the nursery chair with seven pounds of increasingly grumpy, hungry baby in her arms. Opening the front fastening of her passion-killer cotton nightgown, she settled Chloe at her breast and James walked in.

He was wearing a pair of dark boxer shorts and carrying a glass of steaming hot milk on a tray. Her heart jumped. His body was as magnificent as she remembered. It hurt to be reminded; she knew every inch of him so intimately. Couldn't he guess how difficult this was for her?

Holding her breath, she waited for that look of distaste, wondering how she would cope with it for a second time. It didn't come. He put the tray near her feet, where she could reach it.

'I heard her crying and you lumbering around like an elephant on drugs.'

His tone was so dry, his description so accurate she wanted to giggle. 'I'm sorry you were woken,' she said, straight-faced. His hair was rumpled, sticking up in tufts, soft strands falling over his forehead, his jawline dark with stubble. She loved him so much. She couldn't help it. As soon as he'd gone—and that could be as soon as tomorrow—she'd begin the long, painful haul of trying to forget him all over again. That promise to herself was uncomforting, the outcome dubious.

'Don't be,' he answered tonelessly. 'That's what I'm here for. To help out. I admit I don't know much about these things, but I imagine a nursing mother needs to drink plenty.'

No revulsion there, not a scrap of it. Maybe she'd been mistaken earlier, she thought as she watched the play of strong muscles across his naked back when he bent to tidy away all the baby paraphernalia.

Better not to watch, to look at him as little as possible. Better too to ask the question, find out for sure. Because as sure as fishes had fins Fiona wouldn't take kindly to be left kicking her heels over the Christmas period.

'I suppose you'll be heading back to London in the morning?' She eased herself to her feet. Her baby daughter had fallen asleep while feeding. But she herself was wide awake now. She was stingingly awake; every nerve-end pricked as she waited for his answer.

He straightened, putting the things on top of a pretty pine cupboard. 'You suppose wrong. I'll be around until I'm satisfied you're coping.'

Relief made her dizzy. He did care. This time he wasn't going to put Fiona before the needs of his estranged wife and baby. Emboldened, she asked softly, 'Would you like to hold her? You won't wake her. I guess she'll sleep until she's hungry again.'

'No.' His answer was unequivocal. But his explanation made her heart twist sharply inside her. 'We lead separate lives, so separate that I wonder if Emily hadn't kept me informed I would ever have known the birth date, the sex of the baby.'

'I would have told you through the solicitors—' Mattie broke in, appalled that he should have thought otherwise. He would have been informed of the birth and she would have waited for his response, hoping against hope that he would claim a father's right to see his child.

But he wasn't listening; he went on tersely, as if she hadn't spoken at all. 'That being the case, I can't afford to get attached to a child whose mother has a tendency to drop off the face of the earth.'

'I would never stop you seeing Chloe,' Mattie stated with breathy urgency. Why would she, when having James accept his daughter had been her dearest, seemingly unattainable wish? 'It would be far better for her to know her father, spend time with him, holidays, even, when she gets older. You must see that.'

'No, why should I? Six months ago you didn't ask what my wishes were, let alone fall in with them. Why the hell should I fall in with yours now?'

He turned for the door, the long muscles in his back tense. 'Think about it, Mattie. And for pity's sake, get some sleep while you can.'

CHAPTER TWELVE

THANK heaven she had a contented baby. At least, it was a case of so far so good, Mattie thought as she tucked Chloe up in her crib after her early morning feed. She would have been fit for nothing but the knacker's yard if she'd had to pace the floor all night with a screaming bundle of red-faced infant fury.

As it was she felt like a limp lettuce. Half the night had been spent wondering about what he'd said and the other half wondering about what he hadn't said. And the whole night knowing he was in her spare room, with her aching to slide into the double bed beside him, beg him to take her in his arms and hold her. Just hold her.

It was only just getting light but she could hear him moving around downstairs as she padded to the bathroom to take a shower. She could picture him making a fire, trudging through the snow to the wood-shed to bring in more fuel, perhaps making a start on breakfast.

James would be doing what he would see as his duty because he was that type of man. After all, she was still his wife, and she'd just given birth to his baby. Her parents would have asked him to look out for her for a little while, then taken off, leaving him with no option but to stay for a few days.

But his face would be tight with irritation. He'd be bored out of his skull, wanting to get back to civilisation. And Fiona.

Not wanting to set eyes on another voluminous maternity dress, much less wanting to wear one, she'd picked out one of the pairs of jeans she'd practically lived in before she'd got too huge, and a bright-coloured sweatshirt to wear on top. If she couldn't squeeze into them she'd just have to go back to those shapeless jogging pants.

Thankfully, the jeans fitted. Just. She felt marginally better. And much better when she brushed her newly washed hair and left it loose around her shoulders, then carefully applied make-up, something she hadn't bothered with for months.

At least it disguised the havoc of a practically sleepless night. Sleepless, thinking of him. Of what he'd said. He'd accused her of not asking what his wishes were, and he'd been right. She hadn't. Why should she have done when she'd already known what they were?

He'd told her himself that he didn't want children, and if that weren't enough Fiona had confirmed it without having been asked. So getting his knickers in a twist because she hadn't meekly asked what his wishes were made him one big hypocrite.

Yet, on the up side, he'd shown genuine feeling when he'd said he couldn't afford to bond with his baby because her mother might disappear off the face of the earth again. Somehow she was going to have to reassure him that that wouldn't happen, that she would be happy for him to make time for his child in his life.

Her mouth set in a determined line, she set off down the twisty, uncarpeted oak staircase, pushed open the door at the bottom and froze, her eyes going wide.

A fire was blazing in the hearth. She'd been right about that but wrong about everything else. He didn't look even vaguely irritated or bored out of his skull. He was grinning at her reaction to what she was seeing.

A dream of a Christmas tree stood just to one side of one of the windows, gold and silver satin-finish baubles caught and reflected the glow of firelight, scarlet satin ribbons twined through the dark green branches and the touches of artificial snow were as glittery as the real stuff she could see outside.

The sun was rising, turning her garden, the fields and woods beyond into a magical fairyland, the sky a thin, pale blue. A perfect Christmas morning. If only everything weren't so wrong.

Tears stung the backs of her eyes. 'It's beautiful,' she said huskily. She wanted to tell him he was beautiful too. Wearing narrow-fitting dark jeans topped by a chunky Aran sweater, his dark hair rumpled, the austerity of his features erased by that charismatic white grin, his eyes smiling for her, made him her idea of male perfection.

She said instead, controlling the wobble in her voice by sheer will-power, 'Where did the tree come from?'

'Dorchester. I had things to do yesterday afternoon, remember? The tree was one of them. The bits and bobs another. I wanted to surprise you. Hey—' his voice flattened '—don't go weepy on me. It's Christmas Day, it's special so we pretend to be happy, OK? Though I did read that new mothers tend to live near the waterworks!'

Had he really taken an interest in the subject? Had he actually read books on pregnancy, childbirth and the aftermath? Somehow she couldn't imagine it. And his 'pretend to be happy' had struck a sour note.

But he was determined to do his part, if the beautifully decorated tree was anything to go by, and when he asked, 'Is Chloe asleep?' she decided she would pretend, too, even if it killed her.

'Soundly. And I have the baby alarm.' Her sudden smile was dazzling, unforced. He had actually called his daughter by her name, for the very first time. Things were definitely looking up in that department. Somehow she was going to have to convince him that she would never, ever deny him access to his child. But carefully. It would be terrible if she frightened him out of the beginnings of parental interest and concern.

'The tree was a lovely surprise,' she told him. 'You must have been up for hours. So you relax while I make breakfast.'

'Sounds good to me.'

He followed her into the kitchen and she had mixed feelings about that. If he'd stayed in the sitting room she would have had a breathing space.

She could be what she was, a single parent, working her way round the needs of her child. On the other hand, and probably stupidly, she wanted to have every moment of time with him that was on offer. A commodity that wouldn't be hers to have for very much longer. A day or so.

She didn't ask what he wanted, she knew. She slid rashers of bacon and tomato halves under the grill, opened a carton of orange juice and put bread in the toaster. Putting a mug of fresh coffee down on the table in front of him, she avoided his eyes. This pretence was beginning to embarrass her and she would have thought that he, more than anybody, would have wanted to cut through to the nitty-gritty, get the details of the divorce settled.

She turned back to the cooker. Perhaps she should be the one to get real, tell him what she'd wanted to say before Fiona had turned her away. That when the divorce came through she would claim nothing in the way of a settlement, that she hoped they could remain friends. Distant friends.

But when he said, 'You're pretty capable around the kitchen these days,' the warmth of his approval made her feel as if her insides were melting.

Reality could wait. It was good to feel as if they were back in the old days, as if they were friends, even if it was only down to paying lip service to this special day. Even opposing armed forces had been known to call a truce on Christmas Day.

'You ain't seen nothin' yet!' she quipped, dividing the bacon and tomatoes equally onto the plates she'd put in the warming oven. 'I even fathomed out how to change a fuse. And unblock a drain.' She handed him his plate and slid into the chair opposite him. 'And I know you're not going to believe this, but I can even use the washing machine without constantly referring to the book of words!'

Was she trying to tell him that she could manage on her own, that she'd changed, that she was no longer a complete idiot where the practicalities of ordinary day-to-day living were concerned? Maybe. Whatever, he didn't appear to take her new independence amiss, emphasising his acceptance when he asked, 'You're working again?'

'Yes, but I don't take on as much as I used to. Just enough to keep me solvent without touching

capital. I couldn't work full-time before Chloe was
born—' she didn't know why she was saying all this,
her tongue was running away with her and she
couldn't stop it '—because there was so much to do
around the cottage, and the garden—'

'Yes, I know. Emily told me. And I was relieved
to hear that you got that retired farm worker in to do
the heavy stuff—digging, painting ceilings, that sort
of thing.'

He'd finished eating, was looking at her with unreadable eyes and Mattie's stomach flipped over.
He'd kept close tabs on her through the past six
months. Emily had relayed all the little details. It
could only mean that he did still care something for
her, that he had felt some sense of responsibility
when she'd believed he'd washed his hands of her
entirely.

It made her feel warm all over, so warm and relaxed that when he said, 'You've made an enviable
home here. How did you find it?' the warmth over-
flowed into a low gurgle of laughter.

'Believe it or not, before I left London I bought
that second-hand elderly Ford and a map. I meant to
head north.' She wasn't going to say that she'd intended to get as far away from him as she could
without leaving England. She wouldn't risk shattering this easy, relaxed mood. 'I reached Dorchester
before I realised I was going the wrong way. I
couldn't bear the thought of turning round, so I
stayed. I found the cottage through a letting agency.'

His mouth twitched and his eyes were dancing
with laughter. 'That figures! You mean to go north
and you end up almost as far south as you can get—
your sense of direction was always nil. Instruct you

to turn left, and you invariably made a right! Matts,'
he said, serious now, 'I worry about you, I really do.
Put you behind the wheel of a car and anything can
happen.'

Mattie's eyes glowed. She didn't have to pretend
to be happy now. He'd said he worried about her. It
had to mean she still did mean something to him.
The feelings he'd once had for her, based on friendship, long association and male lust, weren't completely dead.

Hope, long atrophied, began to bloom. Maybe
things between him and Fiona hadn't worked out—
which would explain why he didn't mind spending
Christmas away from London. Maybe he wanted his
wife back. Why else had he gone to the trouble of
providing a tree if it hadn't been to impress her?

She would never be the love of his life, she knew
that, but maybe, for Chloe's sake, they could make
their marriage work.

If he did want her back, could she forgive his in-
fidelity?

The answer to that was a sobering 'Yes'. She had
loved him for so long that she would do anything,
forgive anything, to be part of his life again.

Her eyes followed him; was she reading too much
into this? He had left the breakfast table and was
taking something from the dresser. Hope was such a
scary thing, it could be so easily shattered. She was
going to have to ask if he wanted her back in his
life. Find out what had happened between him and
Fiona. She couldn't bear not knowing.

But he forestalled her. He put a large brown envelope down on the table in front of her and stood
behind her. 'For you. Happy Christmas, Matts.'

There was a flatness about his voice that worried her. A sense of foreboding settled around her heart and her fingers shook slightly as she lifted the flap and withdrew the documents.

She was holding the deeds to the cottage, in her name, and she was glad he was behind her and couldn't see the sheer desolation in her eyes.

'How generous.' Her voice was hard and tight. Of course he didn't want her back. He wanted her here, out of his way. He was salving his conscience by making sure she had her own roof over her head.

She'd been such a fool to hope it had been otherwise. Worse than a fool. A total wimp, willing to do anything to stay with a man who didn't want her.

Despicable!

'Not at all.' She heard the tug of his indrawn breath. 'When I heard you'd fallen in love with this place and were happy making a home here, I contacted the owner and made him an offer he couldn't refuse. Knowing you, I didn't expect you'd have the common sense to have a watertight lease drawn up. I didn't want you, or the child, to be thrown out on a landlord's whim.'

'How thoughtful.' The acid in her tone would have etched through rock. She pushed the deeds back into the envelope, stood up and moved away from him. She was on her own now. She had to be strong.

But she didn't feel strong. She felt nauseous. His presence had turned her into a child crying for the moon, always wanting something she could never have.

'Mattie.' His voice flowed over her, tugged at something deep inside her. She turned unwillingly. While he was here she would never get back to being the sane and sensible woman who had made a whole new life for herself. Somehow she would have to make him go.

'Do you really want a divorce?'

The look in his eyes, the soft tone of his question, tore her to pieces.

Of course she didn't want a divorce! In a perfect world divorce was the very last thing she wanted. But this was far from being a perfect world. Fiona was in it. And she wasn't going to hope that he wanted her to say so. No way would she go down that track again, and if she was even remotely tempted she only had to look at that brown envelope on the table!

'Yes,' she said.

'I see.' His face went rigid.

Mattie pulled in a deep breath. Everything inside her was shaking in reaction. 'I think it would be better if you left as soon as the roads are passable.'

He folded his arms across his chest. He looked like a man who was definitely staying put. 'Just tell me one thing. Why?' His voice was abrasive. 'One minute you seemed to be perfectly happy, the next you were telling me you were pregnant and wanted a divorce. And the next thing I knew you'd high-tailed it to God knows where,' he added bitterly.

'I would have thought that was obvious!' she flung at him, all the pain she had suffered making her voice harsh. 'I knew you didn't want children, and I knew why because you'd told me. And I knew what would happen if I got pregnant because Fiona told me. You'd throw me out! So I got in there first! And I knew it was her you wanted, not me. You didn't waste a second before you moved her in.'

For a split second there was a deathly silence, and then he said, his face white with anger, 'My God, your opinion of me is rock-bottom, isn't it? You think me capable of that?'

His hands were bunched into fists at his side, as if he was having a hard time stopping himself from punching the wall. Mattie had never seen him so angry. 'Just as yesterday you thought I'd left you here to cope alone? Or was all that garbage just a convenient excuse?' His mouth tightened and the coldness of his eyes withered her soul. 'I was right all along, wasn't I? There are names for women like you, women who take, and scarper when they've got all they want. But you were right in one thing, it's past time I went. I just hope you can live with yourself!'

'James!'

But he'd gone. She heard the front door slam. She wanted to run after him, to ask him to explain what he'd meant. Her legs wouldn't function, though, giving way beneath her. She sank to the floor and buried her head in her hands.

Had she read everything wrong? Had what she'd seen, heard and deduced been nothing but an illusion? Had she lost the only chance of happiness she would ever have?

CHAPTER THIRTEEN

MINUTES later, when Mattie heard the outer door open and close again she got heavily to her feet, her heart thudding painfully. James. It couldn't be anyone else.

She expected to hear him going upstairs to collect his gear. He'd been in such a blistering rage he would have forgotten the things he was leaving behind. It would save her the trouble of sending them on, she thought dully.

But the door to the kitchen opened. Mattie couldn't look at him; she hadn't the strength. She had never felt so drained, so dispirited, in all of her life.

The silence was like a heavy grey blanket. She couldn't bear it. Keeping her eyes on the debris of what had been a cheerful breakfast—with laughter, even, over her abysmal sense of direction—she mumbled, 'Forgotten something?'

'My common sense,' he came back heavily. 'One of us has to access some of the stuff. You never had much at the best of times and mine got flooded out by emotion. Which, I might tell you, is something of a first.'

Emotion? If he was talking about his white-hot rage then it was an emotion she could do without. She couldn't take any more. Wearily, she began to clear the table, her fingers clumsy.

'Leave that.' In a series of loping strides he was

at her side, relieving her of the tottery pile of cups and saucers. 'Sit down while I make coffee. We could both use a cup.'

In a few deft movements he had cleared the table, leaving the baby alarm and the wretched brown envelope that cruelly reminded her that he had no intention of having her or their baby back in his life. And what common sense had to do with anything, she was too burned out to try to imagine.

Mattie could hear him stacking the dishes in the sink, running hot water over them. The kettle was coming to the boil. She didn't know how he could concentrate on practicalities when everything was so dreadful.

But the mug of hot black coffee he put down in front of her did seem like a good idea. She pushed at the lock of hair that had fallen over her face with the back of one hand as he took the chair opposite. His mouth was straight, his jawline determined, but the silver glitter of his eyes told of some internal battle.

She knew it was a battle he would win when he told her, 'Logic—not emotion—that's what I work on, you know that. Mattie, when you sprang pregnancy and divorce on me in the space of two seconds I was shell-shocked. Then logic kicked in, told me to let you sleep on it, simmer down, and we could talk rationally in the morning. But by then, of course, you'd gone.'

She shuddered. She didn't want to go over this. It was in the past; she'd spent the last six months putting it there. She cradled the coffee-mug in both hands and he said, 'Well? Nothing to say? Look, I'm going to get to the bottom of what went on inside your head, so let's push it along, shall we? If our daughter stays asleep for another ten minutes we might just get there.'

Nothing but soft little snuffles came from the baby listener. Mattie almost wished for a hungry wail to give her the excuse to get out of the corner he'd pushed her into. Unfortunately, he seemed to take her tongue-tied silence for a willingness to be marched down a road she didn't want to travel.

'I've waited for this for six long, hard months, and I'll be damned if I'll wait any longer. I've known where you were, ever since you settled. But I didn't come demanding answers for the same reason I'd had your father pass on my letters—I was afraid you'd take off again. So I waited. Waited until I'd acquired this place in your name, waited until our child was born.'

The look of determination on his strong features told her he wouldn't wait any longer. 'I can't tell you anything you don't already know,' she mumbled defeatedly.

'Try me. No? Then let's come at it from a different direction. Out there, ten minutes ago, I was set to break all records back to London—snow or no snow. Do you know what stopped me?'

Mutely Mattie shook her head. How should she know? He probably wanted to bawl her out some more, and she simply couldn't take it.

'I've had months to look at the facts, and that's what I'm good at,' he said flatly. 'I came up with two possible explanations. One, you were financially secure—the trust fund Edward set up for you years ago, the shares in the business, your earning capability—you didn't need me to provide for you. You'd entered into a marriage of convenience, which had changed. The change meant that you conceived a child. So you left, having got what you now knew you wanted—the baby I'd let you believe you would never have.'

He impaled her with steely eyes. 'Or two, Fiona had something to do with it. Her name kept cropping up. Out there common sense told me that anger wouldn't solve anything. I've known you long enough to be certain you don't have a mean or self-serving bone in your body. You don't make practical, hard-headed decisions unless you're forced to. Your behaviour was driven by emotion. And my guess is it had a lot to do with your low self-esteem and Fiona.'

His matter-of-fact tone hit a raw nerve. Several raw nerves! He thought he was so darned clever, so superior. Patronising beast!

'Too right, it did! I don't know how you dare to think anything else!' Anger injected her with bristling life, put hectic spots of colour on her pale cheeks. 'You've never stopped loving her and don't try to tell me any different. And you'd throw me out like a shot the minute she told you she'd thought things over and didn't mind being childless because you were still crazy about each other. Especially with me being pregnant—you'd do what you'd threatened to do to her. Throw me out! And there the two of you were—laughing and smiling—it made me ill just to look at you!'

She was incoherent, and knew it. There were tears pouring down her face. She wasn't crying, though, of course she wasn't! It was outrage, and anger, and a warped kind of relief to be getting it all off her chest. 'And there she was, the very next morning, wearing something disgustingly small, telling me to go away, I wasn't wanted around the place—and you'd told her to say that, say that our solicitors would deal with everything!'

She gave a huge, inelegant sniff. 'Something to do with Fiona?' she parroted. 'Go right to the top of the class!'

'Mattie, shut up.' He took the mug she was in danger of grinding to dust from her clenched fists, moved it out of harm's way. 'You're not making a whole lot of sense. Just when did this enlightening conversation take place between the two of you?'

His voice had softened. It didn't make the slightest bit of difference. She ground out crossly, 'Where do you think? That charity thing. The one I hadn't wanted to go to because I'd found out I was pregnant and was going to have to tell you, and she comes wiggling up and tells me—'

His finger across her lips was a highly effective silencer. Just the touch of his finger and the wild anger drained right out of her. She was reduced to a quivering mass of near idiocy. She would never get over him. Never!

'I think I'm beginning to get the drift. So straight after that, you saw us together? Sure I was laughing. In her face, right? She was obviously determined to flirt, making the sort of immoral suggestions I won't sully your ears with. And I took enormous pleasure telling her she was wasting her time. I had a wife who satisfied every possible need.'

One straight dark brow quirked upwards. 'And because of what she'd said, you felt bound to ask me if I'd told her I didn't want a family, yes? And because of your inexplicable low self-esteem you frightened yourself into believing that everything she'd said was gospel truth. She'd been trying to break us up, surely you can see that? And she succeeded. You left me and gave me the worst six months of my entire life.'

She gave him a stricken look. 'Do you mean that? Have you really stopped loving her?' Every nerve in her body was as tense as piano wire. She so desperately wanted him to answer in the affirmative, but didn't know if she could believe him if he did.

'I never loved her, Mattie,' he answered soberly. 'It doesn't reflect well on me, but try to understand. I'd reached the conclusion that it was time I settled down, took a wife, someone who would fit in with my lifestyle, a social asset, if you like. I didn't fancy the idea of being completely alone in the years to come. Fiona fitted the bill, or so I thought. I proposed to her with my head, Mattie, not my heart. I told her I wasn't interested in having a family, but she said she had no problem with that. She said she didn't have a maternal bone in her body.'

He shrugged shoulders made even hunkier by the chunky sweater he was wearing. 'She was already beginning to irritate and bore me by the time I overheard her telling some Hooray Henry at a party that she could put up with marrying someone like me providing the income had plenty of noughts behind it. Mattie, despite what she said in that interview she gave to the press, *I* broke the engagement, not the other way around. Do you believe me?'

She wanted to, she really did. But she had to ask, 'Then what was she doing in our home? Delivering the Sunday papers?' She glanced across at him, her mouth sulky, her eyes full of a misery she couldn't hide. 'I knew I'd overreacted, dashing out the way I had. Hormones acting up, I suppose. I came back the following morning so we could talk. She opened the door, with those hateful messages from you.'

His eyes fixed on her face, he reached out and took her hands. Her breath went. The lump of emotion that was stuck in her throat felt as big as Everest. 'I didn't give her any messages to pass on, and that's God's truth,' he told her rawly. 'I had no idea you'd been near the house. You must have arrived when I'd been through at the back. Mrs Briggs had come to me in a panic—the washing machine hose had got blocked and was flooding the place. And Fiona was there because I'd asked her to come—no, don't flinch, Matts.' His fingers tightened around hers. 'Because you'd mentioned her the night before, just before you said you wanted a divorce, I thought the spiteful madam might have had something to do with it and I wanted to know what. I'd seen her talking to you, and after that everything changed. What had been wonderful for us became a nightmare.'

'Was it a nightmare? For you, too?' she asked softly, wondering if she could believe the evidence of her own ears, not quite daring to, not quite yet.

A sudden bleakness clouded his eyes. 'You'd better believe it. I could get nothing out of Fiona and sent her packing. I phoned your father's apartment, left messages—nothing. I had no idea where you were. I was nearly out of my mind when I finally got hold of Edward and he told me you'd been in touch, were safe and well.' His eyes held hers firmly. 'I want you to come back to me.'

There was a moment, just a moment, when elation

flooded through her, leaving her dizzy with joy. Then reality moved in. It wasn't enough, nowhere near enough, not any more.

She gently withdrew her hands from his and stood up. She was steadier now. Stronger. He had never been in love with Fiona, she believed him implicitly. He wasn't capable of giving his heart to anyone. Their baby needed to be loved, and, dammit all, so did she!

She looked at him steadily, refusing to let the lines of strain around his compressed mouth touch her tender heart. She had always loved him and always would. But she couldn't live with him, knowing her love would never be returned. She wouldn't let herself be used again, the way she'd been used before.

'No,' she said quietly. 'There would be too much missing.' She turned away, swallowing hard.

Earlier, much earlier, before she'd come down, he'd put the turkey in a roasting tin ready for the oven. Not a big bird, and he'd put rashers of bacon over the breast. She was being practical and sensible. It was the only way to go forward. She put the bird in the oven. The backs of her eyes stung with unshed tears. She was capable of thinking logically, of doing the right thing.

Straightening, she felt his hands on her shoulders and forced herself to stay rigid, unyielding. She could do it; she knew she could.

He turned her, slowly, and she said woodenly, 'I think we should try to make things as normal as possible, just for today.'

'Explain yourself.' He gave her a gentle shake, his eyes glittering into hers, his breathing shallow.

Briefly closing her eyes, she tried to gather her

strength. Turning him down had been the hardest thing she'd ever had to do. But it had been the right thing. 'It would be a pity to waste good food, we have to eat—'

His hands dropped away. 'Don't push it, Matts,' he advised tersely. 'You know what I mean. Tell me what you think would be missing that wasn't there before.'

Her eyes clashed stubbornly with his before dropping away. She pulled in a raggedy breath. He did deserve to know exactly how she felt. It would draw a line under their relationship. Being all logic and no heart, he would appreciate that.

Sure it would mean letting him know she loved him, and he would feel sorry for her. But she had learned to cope with so many things, she could cope with his pity.

'OK.' She gave a tiny shrug. 'I'll tell you what would be missing. Just bear with me.' She felt old and tired and drainingly unhappy as she crossed the floor to the sink, filled the kettle and plugged it in. She needed the stimulation of more strong, hot coffee and keeping her hands occupied would help her get through this. 'You said you proposed to Fiona with your head,' she reminded him sadly. 'I can understand that. You can't let yourself get emotionally involved because of the way you were brought up. You must have learned very early in your life that loving someone brought the pain of rejection. You programmed any kind of emotion out of your life.'

He said nothing to contradict her, but she hadn't expected him to. She reached two mugs from the Welsh dresser and spooned in coffee granules. 'Being a good man, an honourable man, you were determined never to have children because of the way you are—' Her voice wobbled. She swallowed hard. Then pushed on, 'When you suggested we marry I admit to thinking it was to pay Fiona back for dumping you so publicly. And when—' She pulled in a sharp breath and wished to heaven she hadn't started this. 'When you said you wanted to have sex with me—' God, how cold and clinical that sounded '—I did wonder if you were using me to help you forget her. But that wasn't the case, was it? You never did love her, the way I thought you did, because you couldn't. When you proposed to me, it was with your head, too—'

'No, Mattie,' he interrupted softly. He was directly behind her now. The kettle was boiling its head off. He reached over her and unplugged it. 'You were always in my heart. A soothing presence. Innocent, trusting, unconsciously funny and totally endearing. When I proposed to you it was because I needed everything you were right in my life. Look at me, Mattie, and believe what I say.'

Hardly daring to breathe, let alone think, in case she let her heart rule her head all over again and allow her to think the impossible, she turned reluctantly. He needed a shave, she noted with the part of her brain that was functioning analytically. The dark shadow on the tough jaw made him look dangerously sexy, she thought with the part that was rapidly turning to mush.

He cupped her face tenderly between his two hands. 'Ours was supposed to be a marriage of convenience, two people—two friends who knew, liked and respected each other—rubbing along together for mutual advantage. That was why the subject of our remaining childless cropped up. For all I knew, you might have wanted half a dozen. And I was off women and meaningless sexual relationships,' he told her dryly. 'Only it didn't work out that way, did it? It got to the stage where I couldn't look at you without wanting to make love to you. You were beautiful, addictive, and I was so damned pleased with myself.' His eyes darkened with self-condemnation. 'I was the man who had everything,' he said with flat derision. 'It was only when you left me that I cottoned on to what had happened. I'd fallen deeply, irredeemably in love with you. For the first time ever I'd given my heart. Unreservedly. And you filled it. I couldn't bear the thought of getting through the rest of my life without you.'

The balls of his thumbs were stroking the line of her cheek-bones and there was no doubting the sincerity of his words. A huge wave of happiness engulfed her; it left her weak and shaken, utterly speechless. She could only raise glittering, golden eyes to his as he said unevenly, 'If you really do want a divorce, you can have it. But, Mattie, if you come back to me, you'll be loved more than any woman has been loved before. I promise you that.'

'And Chloe, too?' she questioned raggedly.

She knew his answer would be deeply important, her heart soaring into the stratosphere when he replied succinctly, 'Both the females in my life will have all the love I'm capable of. Can we start over? Please, Mattie?'

She had never seen him look so vulnerable. It would have broken her heart if it hadn't already been bursting with joy. 'Of course we can!' she whispered huskily, then giggled hysterically as an angry wail from the baby alarm broke the magical moment.

With a smothered groan, he caught her to him, pressing her urgently against the solid wall of his chest. But when he released her he was grinning. 'I guess this is what being a parent is all about! Stay right where you are, I'll fetch her. And then I'll tell you how happy you've made me!'

He loped to the door, his energy suddenly boundless, and she followed, calling after him as he pounded up the twisty stairs. 'James, I love you, too. I always did!'

Every last doubt about his commitment to his baby daughter was swept away as she watched the way he descended the stairs so carefully moments later. Chloe was held next to his heart, her downy head tucked under his chin, and his proud and loving smile would have lit the midnight sky.

'I can't offer to feed her,' he said softly as he handed the precious bundle over. 'But I can go and get all those things you seem to need. Mattie, tell me, did you mean what you just said?' he asked as she settled into the corner of the sofa with the now-squirming Chloe. 'You do love me?'

She laid a gentle hand on his cheek. It felt like sandpaper. 'You need a shave.' The look she gave him was shamelessly provocative. 'Of course I love you. How could I not? I've been stuck with it since I wore my hair in pigtails and had legs like knobbly sticks under my gym slip.'

'Thank you,' he said simply and bent to kiss the side of her mouth, running a forefinger down the swollen side of her breast and the suckling baby's velvety cheek. 'Thank you for that.'

One moment he was there, cocooning her and their baby with his love, the next she could hear him moving around upstairs and when he came down again he looked sheepish.

'I brought this.' The carry-cot, piled high with all the baby-changing paraphernalia he had been able to lay his hands on. 'I thought if she slept down here we could share her first Christmas Day with her. And I could show her the tree, and I could change her while you baste the turkey. I've got to learn, haven't I?'

'She's all yours.' Mattie couldn't stop smiling as she handed the infant over. The baby gave a satisfactory burp against his shoulder and stared at her father with unfocussed blue eyes.

Mattie went through to the kitchen on winged feet. James loved her; he loved their little daughter. She had never been happier in the whole of her life!

The fire was burning low in the hearth. The shiny baubles on the tree reflected the last dancing flame. Chloe was sound asleep in her carry-cot, her rosy lips pursing now and then to blow tiny bubbles.

Mattie snuggled more deeply into James' shoulder, drugged with love. Christmas Day was almost over but the perfection, the magic of it, would stay in their hearts until they were both old and grey. 'James,' she asked sleepily, 'the cottage is ours. What are we going to do with it?'

How silly she'd been to be frightened off by a plain brown envelope. His answer, she knew, would be entirely satisfactory.

It was. 'You know me, I plan for every contingency.' He ran a finger down the neat line of her

nose. 'If you had wanted nothing more to do with
me, I'd at least have known you had a secure home.
But if, as I'd hoped and prayed you would, you came
back to me, then I thought we could build on at the
back—there'd be no problem with planning permission, I checked that—and put Mrs Briggs here as
permanent housekeeper.

'I sounded her out, and she's all for it. We could
come down at weekends, or whenever we wanted to.
Chloe will love the freedom when she gets old
enough to toddle about. We'll find someone younger
and more capable back in London. Someone who can
help you with any entertaining we need to do and
turn her hand to babysitting when we need her to.
I'm not going to let you wear yourself to a frazzle.
You and I have a lot of living to do.'

'And loving.' She smothered a yawn. 'You really
do have an answer to everything, don't you?'

'You'd better believe it. On both counts. Bedtime,
Mrs Carter.' He stood up, taking both her hands and
drawing her to her feet. He folded her into his arms.
'I'm going to hold you all night,' he said, his voice
thick with love. 'And if the little lady gets hungry
and wakes, I'll fetch her to you. And do the changing
bit. And bring you breakfast in bed in the morning.
How does that sound?'

'Bliss,' she said, her head against his heart, her
arms twining around his neck. 'Utter, perfect bliss!'

HARLEQUIN® *Presents*

The world's bestselling romance series. Seduction and passion guaranteed!

Pick up a Harlequin Presents® novel and you will enter a world of spine-tingling passion and provocative, tantalizing romance!

Join us in 2002 for an exciting selection of titles from all your favorite authors:

Red Hot Revenge
COLE CAMERON'S REVENGE #2223, January
by Sandra Marton

Secret Passions
A truly thrilling new duet
THE SECRET VENGEANCE #2236, March
THE SECRET LOVE CHILD #2242, April
by Miranda Lee

A Mediterranean Marriage
THE BELLINI BRIDE #2224, January
by Michelle Reid
and
THE ITALIAN'S WIFE #2235, March
by Lynne Graham

An upbeat, contemporary story
THE CITY-GIRL BRIDE #2229, February
by Penny Jordan

An involving and dramatic read
A RICH MAN'S TOUCH #2230, February
by Anne Mather

On sale in the New Year
Available wherever Harlequin Books are sold.

HARLEQUIN®
Makes any time special ®

Visit us at www.eHarlequin.com

HPDECPRE

Who needs Cupid when you've got kids?

Sealed with a Kiss

A delightful collection
from *New York Times*
Bestselling Author

DEBBIE MACOMBER

JUDITH BOWEN

HELEN BROOKS

Romance and laughter abound as
the matchmaking efforts of some
very persistent children bring
true love to their parents.

HARLEQUIN®
Makes any time special ®

Available in January 2002...just in time for Valentine's Day!

Visit us at www.eHarlequin.com

PHSK

Pick up a Harlequin Presents® novel and enter a world of spine-tingling passion and provocative, tantalizing romance!

Join us in December for two sexy Italian heroes from two of your favorite authors:

RAFAELLO'S MISTRESS
by Lynne Graham
#2217

THE ITALIAN'S RUNAWAY BRIDE
by Jacqueline Baird
#2219

HARLEQUIN
Presents

The world's bestselling romance series.

Seduction and passion guaranteed.

Available wherever Harlequin books are sold.

Visit us at www.eHarlequin.com
HPITAL

If you enjoyed what you just read,
then we've got an offer you can't resist!

Take 2 bestselling love stories FREE!

Plus get a FREE surprise gift!

Clip this page and mail it to Harlequin Reader Service®

IN U.S.A.	IN CANADA
3010 Walden Ave.	P.O. Box 609
P.O. Box 1867	Fort Erie, Ontario
Buffalo, N.Y. 14240-1867	L2A 5X3

YES! Please send me 2 free Harlequin Presents® novels and my free surprise gift. After receiving them, if I don't wish to receive anymore, I can return the shipping statement marked cancel. If I don't cancel, I will receive 6 brand-new novels every month, before they're available in stores! In the U.S.A., bill me at the bargain price of $3.34 plus 25¢ shipping & handling per book and applicable sales tax, if any*. In Canada, bill me at the bargain price of $3.74 plus 25¢ shipping & handling per book and applicable taxes**. That's the complete price and a savings of at least 10% off the cover prices—what a great deal! I understand that accepting the 2 free books and gift places me under no obligation ever to buy any books. I can always return a shipment and cancel at any time. Even if I never buy another book from Harlequin, the 2 free books and gift are mine to keep forever.

106 HEN DFNY
306 HEN DC7T

Name	(PLEASE PRINT)	
Address	Apt.#	
City	State/Prov.	Zip/Postal Code

* Terms and prices subject to change without notice. Sales tax applicable in N.Y.
** Canadian residents will be charged applicable provincial taxes and GST.
  All orders subject to approval. Offer limited to one per household and not valid to
  current Harlequin Presents® subscribers..
  ® are registered trademarks of Harlequin Enterprises Limited.

PRES01   ©2001 Harlequin Enterprises Limited

Together for the first time
in one Collector's Edition!

New York Times bestselling authors

Barbara Delinsky

Catherine Coulter

Linda Howard

Forever Yours

**A special trade-size volume containing three
complete novels that showcase the passion,
imagination and stunning power that these
talented authors are famous for.**

Coming to your favorite retail outlet in December 2001.

HARLEQUIN®
Makes any time special®

Visit us at www.eHarlequin.com   PHFY

HARLEQUIN® Presents~

Passion™

Looking for stories that **sizzle**?

Wanting a read that has a little extra **spice**?

Harlequin Presents® is thrilled to bring you romances that turn up the **heat**!

Every other month there'll be a **PRESENTS PASSION™** book by one of your favorite authors.

Pick up a **PRESENTS PASSION™**— where **seduction** is guaranteed!

Available wherever Harlequin books are sold.

HARLEQUIN®
Makes any time special ®

Visit us at www.eHarlequin.com   INTPASS

CALL THE ONES YOU LOVE OVER THE HOLIDAYS!

Save $25 off future book purchases when you buy any four Harlequin® or Silhouette® books in October, November and December 2001,

PLUS

receive a phone card good for 15 minutes of long-distance calls to anyone you want in North America!

WHAT AN INCREDIBLE DEAL!

Just fill out this form and attach 4 proofs of purchase (cash register receipts) from October, November and December 2001 books, and Harlequin Books will send you a coupon booklet worth a total savings of $25 off future purchases of Harlequin® and Silhouette® books, AND a 15-minute phone card to call the ones you love, anywhere in North America.

Please send this form, along with your cash register receipts as proofs of purchase, to:
In the USA: Harlequin Books, P.O. Box 9057, Buffalo, NY 14269-9057
In Canada: Harlequin Books, P.O. Box 622, Fort Erie, Ontario L2A 5X3
Cash register receipts must be dated no later than December 31, 2001.
Limit of 1 coupon booklet and phone card per household.
Please allow 4-6 weeks for delivery.

**I accept your offer! Enclosed are 4 proofs of purchase.
Please send me my coupon booklet
and a 15-minute phone card:**

Name: _____

Address: _____ City: _____

State/Prov.: _____ Zip/Postal Code: _____

Account Number (if available): _____

---

097 KJB DAGL
PHQ4013